William Butler Yeats

Poems Lyrical and Narrative

Outlook

William Butler Yeats

Poems Lyrical and Narrative

1. Auflage | ISBN: 978-3-73261-859-0

Erscheinungsort: Paderborn, Deutschland

Erscheinungsjahr: 2018

Outlook Verlag GmbH, Paderborn.

William Butler Yeats

Poems Lyrical and Narrative

Outlook

THE COLLECTED WORKS OF WILLIAM BUTLER YEATS

From a charcoal drawing by John S. Sargent, R. A.

POEMS LYRICAL AND NARRATIVE
BEING THE FIRST VOLUME OF
THE
COLLECTED WORKS IN VERSE
AND
PROSE OF WILLIAM BUTLER
YEATS
IMPRINTED AT THE
SHAKESPEARE
HEAD PRESS STRATFORD-ON-
AVON
MCMVIII

THE WIND AMONG THE REEDS

THE HOSTING OF THE SIDHE

The host is riding from Knocknarea

And over the grave of Clooth-na-bare;

Caolte tossing his burning hair

And Niamh calling *Away, come away:*

Empty your heart of its mortal dream.

The winds awaken, the leaves whirl round,

Our cheeks are pale, our hair is unbound,

Our breasts are heaving, our eyes are a-gleam,

Our arms are waving, our lips are apart;

And if any gaze on our rushing band,

We come between him and the deed of his hand,

We come between him and the hope of his heart.

The host is rushing 'twixt night and day,

And where is there hope or deed as fair?

Caolte tossing his burning hair,

And Niamh calling *Away, come away.*

THE EVERLASTING VOICES

O sweet everlasting Voices, be still;

Go to the guards of the heavenly fold

And bid them wander obeying your will

Flame under flame, till Time be no more;

Have you not heard that our hearts are old,

That you call in birds, in wind on the hill,

In shaken boughs, in tide on the shore?

O sweet everlasting Voices, be still.

THE MOODS

Tɪᴍᴇ drops in decay,
Like a candle burnt out,
And the mountains and woods
Have their day, have their day;
What one in the rout
Of the fire-born moods
Has fallen away?

THE LOVER TELLS OF THE ROSE IN HIS HEART

Aʟʟ things uncomely and broken, all things worn out and old,
The cry of a child by the roadway, the creak of a lumbering cart,
The heavy steps of the ploughman, splashing the wintry mould,
Are wronging your image that blossoms a rose in the deeps of my heart.
The wrong of unshapely things is a wrong too great to be told;
I hunger to build them anew and sit on a green knoll apart,
With the earth and the sky and the water, remade, like a casket of gold
For my dreams of your image that blossoms a rose in the deeps of my heart.

THE HOST OF THE AIR

O'Dʀɪꜱᴄᴏʟʟ drove with a song
The wild duck and the drake
From the tall and the tufted reeds
Of the drear Hart Lake.
And he saw how the reeds grew dark
At the coming of night tide,
And dreamed of the long dim hair
Of Bridget his bride.
He heard while he sang and dreamed
A piper piping away,

And never was piping so sad,

And never was piping so gay.

And he saw young men and young girls

Who danced on a level place

And Bridget his bride among them,

With a sad and a gay face.

The dancers crowded about him,

And many a sweet thing said,

And a young man brought him red wine

And a young girl white bread.

But Bridget drew him by the sleeve,

Away from the merry bands,

To old men playing at cards

With a twinkling of ancient hands.

The bread and the wine had a doom,

For these were the host of the air;

He sat and played in a dream

Of her long dim hair.

He played with the merry old men

And thought not of evil chance,

Until one bore Bridget his bride

Away from the merry dance.

He bore her away in his arms,

The handsomest young man there,

And his neck and his breast and his arms

Were drowned in her long dim hair.

O'Driscoll scattered the cards

And out of his dream awoke:

Old men and young men and young girls

Were gone like a drifting smoke;

But he heard high up in the air A

piper piping away,

And never was piping so sad,

And never was piping so gay.

THE FISHERMAN

Aɭᴛʜᴏᴜɢʜ you hide in the ebb and flow

Of the pale tide when the moon has set,

The people of coming days will know

About the casting out of my net,

And how you have leaped times out of mind

Over the little silver cords,

And think that you were hard and unkind,

And blame you with many bitter words.

A CRADLE SONG

Tʜᴇ Danaan children laugh, in cradles of wrought gold,

And clap their hands together, and half close their eyes,

For they will ride the North when the ger-eagle flies,

With heavy whitening wings, and a heart fallen cold:

I kiss my wailing child and press it to my breast, And

hear the narrow graves calling my child and me.

Desolate winds that cry over the wandering sea;

Desolate winds that hover in the flaming West;

Desolate winds that beat the doors of Heaven, and beat

The doors of Hell and blow there many a whimpering ghost;

O heart the winds have shaken; the unappeasable host

Is comelier than candles at Mother Mary's feet.

INTO THE TWILIGHT

Out-worn heart, in a time out-worn,
Come clear of the nets of wrong and right;
Laugh, heart, again in the gray twilight,
Sigh, heart, again in the dew of the morn.
Your mother Eire is always young,
Dew ever shining and twilight gray;
Though hope fall from you and love decay,
Burning in fires of a slanderous tongue.
Come, heart, where hill is heaped upon hill
For there the mystical brotherhood
Of sun and moon and hollow and wood
And river and stream work out their will;
And God stands winding His lonely horn,
And time and the world are ever in flight;
And love is less kind than the gray twilight
And hope is less dear than the dew of the morn.

THE SONG OF WANDERING AENGUS

I went out to the hazel wood,
Because a fire was in my head,
And cut and peeled a hazel wand,
And hooked a berry to a thread;
And when white moths were on the wing,
And moth-like stars were flickering out,
I dropped the berry in a stream
And caught a little silver trout.
When I had laid it on the floor
I went to blow the fire a-flame,
But something rustled on the floor,
And someone called me by my name:

It had become a glimmering girl
With apple blossom in her hair
Who called me by my name and ran
And faded through the brightening air.
Though I am old with wandering
Through hollow lands and hilly lands,
I will find out where she has gone,
And kiss her lips and take her hands;
And walk among long dappled grass,
And pluck till time and times are done
The silver apples of the moon,
The golden apples of the sun.

THE HEART OF THE WOMAN

O WHAT to me the little room
That was brimmed up with prayer and rest;
He bade me out into the gloom,
And my breast lies upon his breast.
O what to me my mother's care,
The house where I was safe and warm;
The shadowy blossom of my hair
Will hide us from the bitter storm.
O hiding hair and dewy eyes,
I am no more with life and death,
My heart upon his warm heart lies,
My breath is mixed into his breath.

THE LOVER MOURNS FOR THE LOSS OF LOVE

PALE brows, still hands and dim hair,
I had a beautiful friend

And dreamed that the old despair

Would end in love in the end:

She looked in my heart one day

And saw your image was there;

She has gone weeping away.

HE MOURNS FOR THE CHANGE THAT HAS COME UPON HIM AND HIS BELOVED AND LONGS FOR THE END OF THE WORLD

Do you not hear me calling, white deer with no horns!

I have been changed to a hound with one red ear;

I have been in the Path of Stones and the Wood of Thorns,

For somebody hid hatred and hope and desire and fear

Under my feet that they follow you night and day.

A man with a hazel wand came without sound;

He changed me suddenly; I was looking another way;

And now my calling is but the calling of a hound;

And Time and Birth and Change are hurrying by.

I would that the Boar without bristles had come from the West

And had rooted the sun and moon and stars out of the sky And

lay in the darkness, grunting, and turning to his rest.

HE BIDS HIS BELOVED BE AT PEACE

I HEAR the Shadowy Horses, their long manes a-shake,

Their hoofs heavy with tumult, their eyes glimmering white;

The North unfolds above them clinging, creeping night,

The East her hidden joy before the morning break,

The West weeps in pale dew and sighs passing away,

The South is pouring down roses of crimson fire:

O vanity of Sleep, Hope, Dream, endless Desire,

The Horses of Disaster plunge in the heavy clay:

Beloved, let your eyes half close, and your heart beat

Over my heart, and your hair fall over my breast,

Drowning love's lonely hour in deep twilight of rest,

And hiding their tossing manes and their tumultuous feet.

HE REPROVES THE CURLEW

O, CURLEW, cry no more in the air,

Or only to the waters in the West;

Because your crying brings to my mind

Passion-dimmed eyes and long heavy hair

That was shaken out over my breast:

There is enough evil in the crying of wind.

HE REMEMBERS FORGOTTEN BEAUTY

WHEN my arms wrap you round I press

My heart upon the loveliness

That has long faded from the world;

The jewelled crowns that kings have hurled

In shadowy pools, when armies fled;

The love-tales wrought with silken thread

By dreaming ladies upon cloth

That has made fat the murderous moth;

The roses that of old time were

Woven by ladies in their hair,

The dew-cold lilies ladies bore

Through many a sacred corridor

Where such gray clouds of incense rose

That only the gods' eyes did not close:

For that pale breast and lingering hand

Come from a more dream-heavy land,

A more dream-heavy hour than this;
And when you sigh from kiss to kiss
I hear white Beauty sighing, too,
For hours when all must fade like dew,
All but the flames, and deep on deep,
Throne over throne where in half sleep,
Their swords upon their iron knees,
Brood her high lonely mysteries.

A POET TO HIS BELOVED

I BRING you with reverent hands
The books of my numberless dreams;
White woman that passion has worn
As the tide wears the dove-gray sands,
And with heart more old than the horn
That is brimmed from the pale fire of time:
White woman with numberless dreams
I bring you my passionate rhyme.

HE GIVES HIS BELOVED CERTAIN RHYMES

FASTEN your hair with a golden pin,
And bind up every wandering tress;
I bade my heart build these poor rhymes:
It worked at them, day out, day in,
Building a sorrowful loveliness
Out of the battles of old times.
You need but lift a pearl-pale hand,
And bind up your long hair and sigh;
And all men's hearts must burn and beat;
And candle-like foam on the dim sand,

And stars climbing the dew-dropping sky,

Live but to light your passing feet.

TO MY HEART, BIDDING IT HAVE NO FEAR

B<small>E</small> you still, be you still, trembling heart;

Remember the wisdom out of the old days:

Him who trembles before the flame and the flood,

And the winds that blow through the starry ways,

Let the starry winds and the flame and the flood

Cover over and hide, for he has no part

With the proud, majestical multitude.

THE CAP AND BELLS

T<small>HE</small> jester walked in the garden:

The garden had fallen still;

He bade his soul rise upward

And stand on her window-sill.

It rose in a straight blue garment,

When owls began to call:

It had grown wise-tongued by thinking

Of a quiet and light footfall;

But the young queen would not listen;

She rose in her pale night gown;

She drew in the heavy casement

And pushed the latches down.

He bade his heart go to her,

When the owls called out no more;

In a red and quivering garment

It sang to her through the door.

It had grown sweet-tongued by dreaming,

Of a flutter of flower-like hair;
But she took up her fan from the table
And waved it off on the air.
'I have cap and bells,' he pondered,
'I will send them to her and die';
And when the morning whitened
He left them where she went by.
She laid them upon her bosom,
Under a cloud of her hair,
And her red lips sang them a love-song:
Till stars grew out of the air.
She opened her door and her window,
And the heart and the soul came through,
To her right hand came the red one,
To her left hand came the blue.
They set up a noise like crickets,
A chattering wise and sweet,
And her hair was a folded flower
And the quiet of love in her feet.

THE VALLEY OF THE BLACK PIG

THE dews drop slowly and dreams gather: unknown spears
Suddenly hurtle before my dream-awakened eyes,
And then the clash of fallen horsemen and the cries
Of unknown perishing armies beat about my ears.
We who still labour by the cromlec on the shore,
The grey cairn on the hill, when day sinks drowned in dew,
Being weary of the world's empires, bow down to you,
Master of the still stars and of the flaming door.

THE LOVER ASKS FORGIVENESS BECAUSE OF HIS MANY MOODS

If this importunate heart trouble your peace

With words lighter than air,

Or hopes that in mere hoping flicker and cease;

Crumple the rose in your hair;

And cover your lips with odorous twilight and say,

'O Hearts of wind-blown flame!

O Winds, elder than changing of night and day,

That murmuring and longing came,

From marble cities loud with tabors of old

In dove-gray faery lands;

From battle banners, fold upon purple fold,

Queens wrought with glimmering hands;

That saw young Niamh hover with love-lorn face

Above the wandering tide;

And lingered in the hidden desolate place,

Where the last Phœnix died

And wrapped the flames above his holy head;

And still murmur and long:

O Piteous Hearts, changing till change be dead

In a tumultuous song':

And cover the pale blossoms of your breast

With your dim heavy hair,

And trouble with a sigh for all things longing for rest

The odorous twilight there.

HE TELLS OF A VALLEY FULL OF LOVERS

I DREAMED that I stood in a valley, and amid sighs,

For happy lovers passed two by two where I stood;

15

And I dreamed my lost love came stealthily out of the wood
With her cloud-pale eyelids falling on dream-dimmed eyes:
I cried in my dream, *O women, bid the young men lay*
Their heads on your knees, and drown their eyes with your hair,
Or remembering hers they will find no other face fair
Till all the valleys of the world have been withered away.

HE TELLS OF THE PERFECT BEAUTY

O CLOUD-PALE eyelids, dream-dimmed eyes,
The poets labouring all their days
To build a perfect beauty in rhyme
Are overthrown by a woman's gaze
And by the unlabouring brood of the skies:
And therefore my heart will bow, when dew
Is dropping sleep, until God burn time,
Before the unlabouring stars and you.

HE HEARS THE CRY OF THE SEDGE

I WANDER by the edge
Of this desolate lake
Where wind cries in the sedge
Until the axle break
That keeps the stars in their round,
And hands hurl in the deep
The banners of East and West,
And the girdle of light is unbound,
Your breast will not lie by the breast
Of your beloved in sleep.

HE THINKS OF THOSE WHO HAVE SPOKEN EVIL OF HIS BELOVED

HALF close your eyelids, loosen your hair,
And dream about the great and their pride;
They have spoken against you everywhere,
But weigh this song with the great and their pride;
I made it out of a mouthful of air,
Their children's children shall say they have lied.

THE BLESSED

CUMHAL called out, bending his head,
Till Dathi came and stood,
With a blink in his eyes at the cave mouth,
Between the wind and the wood.
And Cumhal said, bending his knees,
'I have come by the windy way
To gather the half of your blessedness
And learn to pray when you pray.
'I can bring you salmon out of the streams
And heron out of the skies.'
But Dathi folded his hands and smiled
With the secrets of God in his eyes.
And Cumhal saw like a drifting smoke
All manner of blessed souls,
Women and children, young men with books,
And old men with croziers and stoles.
'Praise God and God's mother,' Dathi said,
'For God and God's mother have sent
The blessedest souls that walk in the world
To fill your heart with content.'
'And which is the blessedest,' Cumhal said,
'Where all are comely and good?

Is it these that with golden thuribles
Are singing about the wood?'
'My eyes are blinking,' Dathi said,
'With the secrets of God half blind,
But I can see where the wind goes
And follow the way of the wind;
'And blessedness goes where the wind goes,
And when it is gone we are dead;
I see the blessedest soul in the world
And he nods a drunken head.
'O blessedness comes in the night and the day
And whither the wise heart knows;
And one has seen in the redness of wine
The Incorruptible Rose,
'That drowsily drops faint leaves on him
And the sweetness of desire,
While time and the world are ebbing away
In twilights of dew and of fire.'

THE SECRET ROSE

F_{AR} off, most secret, and inviolate Rose,
Enfold me in my hour of hours; where those
Who sought thee in the Holy Sepulchre,
Or in the wine vat, dwell beyond the stir
And tumult of defeated dreams; and deep
Among pale eyelids, heavy with the sleep
Men have named beauty. Thy great leaves enfold
The ancient beards, the helms of ruby and gold
Of the crowned Magi; and the king whose eyes
Saw the Pierced Hands and Rood of elder rise

In Druid vapour and make the torches dim;
Till vain frenzy awoke and he died; and him
Who met Fand walking among flaming dew
By a gray shore where the wind never blew,
And lost the world and Emer for a kiss;
And him who drove the gods out of their liss,
And till a hundred morns had flowered red,
Feasted and wept the barrows of his dead;
And the proud dreaming king who flung the crown
And sorrow away, and calling bard and clown
Dwelt among wine-stained wanderers in deep woods;
And him who sold tillage, and house, and goods,
And sought through lands and islands numberless years,
Until he found with laughter and with tears,
A woman, of so shining loveliness,
That men threshed corn at midnight by a tress,
A little stolen tress. I, too, await
The hour of thy great wind of love and hate.
When shall the stars be blown about the sky,
Like the sparks blown out of a smithy, and die?
Surely thine hour has come, thy great wind blows,
Far off, most secret, and inviolate Rose?

MAID QUIET

Where has Maid Quiet gone to,
Nodding her russet hood?
The winds that awakened the stars
Are blowing through my blood.
O how could I be so calm
When she rose up to depart?

Now words that called up the lightning

Are hurtling through my heart.

THE TRAVAIL OF PASSION

W<small>HEN</small> the flaming lute-thronged angelic door is wide;

When an immortal passion breathes in mortal clay;

Our hearts endure the scourge, the plaited thorns, the way

Crowded with bitter faces, the wounds in palm and side,

The hyssop-heavy sponge, the flowers by Kidron stream:

We will bend down and loosen our hair over you,

That it may drop faint perfume, and be heavy with dew,

Lilies of death-pale hope, roses of passionate dream.

THE LOVER PLEADS WITH HIS FRIEND FOR OLD FRIENDS

T<small>HOUGH</small> you are in your shining days,

Voices among the crowd

And new friends busy with your praise,

Be not unkind or proud,

But think about old friends the most:

Time's bitter flood will rise,

Your beauty perish and be lost

For all eyes but these eyes.

A LOVER SPEAKS TO THE HEARERS OF HIS SONGS IN COMING DAYS

O, <small>WOMEN</small>, kneeling by your altar rails long hence,

When songs I wove for my beloved hide the prayer,

And smoke from this dead heart drifts through the violet air

And covers away the smoke of myrrh and frankincense;

Bend down and pray for the great sin I wove in song,

Till Mary of the wounded heart cry a sweet cry,

And call to my beloved and me: 'No longer fly

Amid the hovering, piteous, penitential throng.'

THE POET PLEADS WITH THE ELEMENTAL POWERS

THE Powers whose name and shape no living creature knows

Have pulled the Immortal Rose;

And though the Seven Lights bowed in their dance and wept,

The Polar Dragon slept,

His heavy rings uncoiled from glimmering deep to deep:

When will he wake from sleep?

Great Powers of falling wave and wind and windy fire,

With your harmonious choir

Encircle her I love and sing her into peace,

That my old care may cease;

Unfold your flaming wings and cover out of sight

The nets of day and night.

Dim Powers of drowsy thought, let her no longer be

Like the pale cup of the sea,

When winds have gathered and sun and moon burned dim

Above its cloudy rim;

But let a gentle silence wrought with music flow

Whither her footsteps go.

HE WISHES HIS BELOVED WERE DEAD

WERE you but lying cold and dead,

And lights were paling out of the West,

You would come hither, and bend your head,

And I would lay my head on your breast;

And you would murmur tender words,

Forgiving me, because you were dead:
Nor would you rise and hasten away,
Though you have the will of the wildbirds,
But know your hair was bound and wound
About the stars and moon and sun:
O would, beloved, that you lay
Under the dock-leaves in the ground,
While lights were paling one by one.

HE WISHES FOR THE CLOTHS OF HEAVEN

H_{AD} I the heavens' embroidered cloths,
Enwrought with golden and silver light,
The blue and the dim and the dark cloths
Of night and light and the half light,
I would spread the cloths under your feet:
But I, being poor, have only my dreams;
I have spread my dreams under your feet;
Tread softly because you tread on my dreams.

HE THINKS OF HIS PAST GREATNESS WHEN A PART OF THE CONSTELLATIONS OF HEAVEN

I _{HAVE} drunk ale from the Country of the Young
And weep because I know all things now:
I have been a hazel tree and they hung
The Pilot Star and the Crooked Plough
Among my leaves in times out of mind:
I became a rush that horses tread:
I became a man, a hater of the wind,
Knowing one, out of all things, alone, that his head
Would not lie on the breast or his lips on the hair

Of the woman that he loves, until he dies;
Although the rushes and the fowl of the air
Cry of his love with their pitiful cries.

THE OLD AGE OF QUEEN MAEVE

MAEVE the great queen was pacing to and fro,
Between the walls covered with beaten bronze,
In her high house at Cruachan; the long hearth,
Flickering with ash and hazel, but half showed
Where the tired horse-boys lay upon the rushes,
Or on the benches underneath the walls,
In comfortable sleep; all living slept
But that great queen, who more than half the night
Had paced from door to fire and fire to door.
Though now in her old age, in her young age
She had been beautiful in that old way
That's all but gone; for the proud heart is gone,
And the fool heart of the counting-house fears all
But soft beauty and indolent desire.
She could have called over the rim of the world
Whatever woman's lover had hit her fancy,
And yet had been great bodied and great limbed,
Fashioned to be the mother of strong children;
And she'd had lucky eyes and a high heart,
And wisdom that caught fire like the dried flax,
At need, and made her beautiful and fierce,
Sudden and laughing.
                    O unquiet heart,
Why do you praise another, praising her,
As if there were no tale but your own tale
Worth knitting to a measure of sweet sound?
Have I not bid you tell of that great queen

Who has been buried some two thousand years?
When night was at its deepest, a wild goose
Cried from the porter's lodge, and with long clamour
Shook the ale horns and shields upon their hooks;
But the horse-boys slept on, as though some power
Had filled the house with Druid heaviness;
And wondering who of the many-changing Sidhe
Had come as in the old times to counsel her,
Maeve walked, yet with slow footfall, being old,
To that small chamber by the outer gate.
The porter slept, although he sat upright
With still and stony limbs and open eyes.
Maeve waited, and when that ear-piercing noise
Broke from his parted lips and broke again,
She laid a hand on either of his shoulders,
And shook him wide awake, and bid him say
Who of the wandering many-changing ones
Had troubled his sleep. But all he had to say
Was that, the air being heavy and the dogs
More still than they had been for a good month,
He had fallen asleep, and, though he had dreamed nothing,
He could remember when he had had fine dreams.
It was before the time of the great war
Over the White-Horned Bull, and the Brown Bull.
She turned away; he turned again to sleep
That no god troubled now, and, wondering
What matters were afoot among the Sidhe,
Maeve walked through that great hall, and with a sigh
Lifted the curtain of her sleeping-room,

Remembering that she too had seemed divine
To many thousand eyes, and to her own
One that the generations had long waited
That work too difficult for mortal hands
Might be accomplished. Bunching the curtain up
She saw her husband Ailell sleeping there,
And thought of days when he'd had a straight body,
And of that famous Fergus, Nessa's husband,
Who had been the lover of her middle life.
Suddenly Ailell spoke out of his sleep,
And not with his own voice or a man's voice,
But with the burning, live, unshaken voice
Of those that it may be can never age.
He said, 'High Queen of Cruachan and Magh Ai,
A king of the Great Plain would speak with you.'
And with glad voice Maeve answered him, 'What king
Of the far wandering shadows has come to me?
As in the old days when they would come and go
About my threshold to counsel and to help.'
The parted lips replied, 'I seek your help,
For I am Aengus, and I am crossed in love.'
'How may a mortal whose life gutters out
Help them that wander with hand clasping hand,
Their haughty images that cannot wither
For all their beauty's like a hollow dream,
Mirrored in streams that neither hail nor rain
Nor the cold North has troubled?'
                              He replied:
'I am from those rivers and I bid you call

The children of the Maines out of sleep,
And set them digging into Anbual's hill.
We shadows, while they uproot his earthy house,
Will overthrow his shadows and carry off
Caer, his blue-eyed daughter that I love.
I helped your fathers when they built these walls,
And I would have your help in my great need,
Queen of high Cruachan.'

                        'I obey your will
With speedy feet and a most thankful heart:
For you have been, O Aengus of the birds,
Our giver of good counsel and good luck.'
And with a groan, as if the mortal breath
Could but awaken sadly upon lips
That happier breath had moved, her husband turned
Face downward, tossing in a troubled sleep;
But Maeve, and not with a slow feeble foot,
Came to the threshold of the painted house,
Where her grandchildren slept, and cried aloud,
Until the pillared dark began to stir
With shouting and the clang of unhooked arms.
She told them of the many-changing ones;
And all that night, and all through the next day
To middle night, they dug into the hill.
At middle night great cats with silver claws,
Bodies of shadow and blind eyes like pearls,
Came up out of the hole, and red-eared hounds
With long white bodies came out of the air
Suddenly, and ran at them and harried them.

The Maines' children dropped their spades, and stood
With quaking joints and terror-strucken faces,
Till Maeve called out: 'These are but common men.
The Maines' children have not dropped their spades,
Because Earth, crazy for its broken power,
Casts up a show and the winds answer it
With holy shadows.' Her high heart was glad,
And when the uproar ran along the grass
She followed with light footfall in the midst,
Till it died out where an old thorn tree stood.
Friend of these many years, you too had stood
With equal courage in that whirling rout;
For you, although you've not her wandering heart,
Have all that greatness, and not hers alone.
For there is no high story about queens
In any ancient book but tells of you;
And when I've heard how they grew old and died,
Or fell into unhappiness, I've said:
'She will grow old and die, and she has wept!'
And when I'd write it out anew, the words,
Half crazy with the thought, She too has wept!
Outrun the measure.
                              I'd tell of that great queen
Who stood amid a silence by the thorn
Until two lovers came out of the air
With bodies made out of soft fire. The one,
About whose face birds wagged their fiery wings,
Said: 'Aengus and his sweetheart give their thanks
To Maeve and to Maeve's household, owing all

In owing them the bride-bed that gives peace.'
Then Maeve: 'O Aengus, Master of all lovers,
A thousand years ago you held high talk
With the first kings of many-pillared Cruachan.
O when will you grow weary?'

                    They had vanished;
But out of the dark air over her head there came
A murmur of soft words and meeting lips.

---

[51]
[52]
[53]

31

BAILE AND AILLINN

Argument. Baile and Aillinn were lovers, but Aengus, the Master of Love, wishing them to be happy in his own land among the dead, told to each a story of the other's death, so that their hearts were broken and they died.

I hardly hear the curlew cry,

Nor the grey rush when the wind is high,

Before my thoughts begin to run

On the heir of Ulad, Buan's son,

Baile, who had the honey mouth;

And that mild woman of the south,

Aillinn, who was King Lugaid's heir.

Their love was never drowned in care

Of this or that thing, nor grew cold

Because their bodies had grown old.

Being forbid to marry on earth,

They blossomed to immortal mirth.

About the time when Christ was born,

When the long wars for the White Horn

And the Brown Bull had not yet come,

Young Baile Honey-Mouth, whom some

Called rather Baile Little-Land,

Rode out of Emain with a band

Of harpers and young men; and they

Imagined, as they struck the way

To many-pastured Muirthemne,

That all things fell out happily,

And there, for all that fools had said,

Baile and Aillinn would be wed.

They found an old man running there:
He had ragged long grass-coloured hair;
He had knees that stuck out of his hose;
He had puddle water in his shoes;
He had half a cloak to keep him dry,
Although he had a squirrel's eye.
O wandering birds and rushy beds,
You put such folly in our heads
With all this crying in the wind;
No common love is to our mind,
And our poor Kate or Nan is less
Than any whose unhappiness
Awoke the harp-strings long ago.
Yet they that know all things but know
That all life had to give us is
A child's laughter, a woman's kiss.
Who was it put so great a scorn
In the grey reeds that night and morn
Are trodden and broken by the herds,
And in the light bodies of birds
That north wind tumbles to and fro
And pinches among hail and snow?
That runner said: 'I am from the south;
I run to Baile Honey-Mouth,
To tell him how the girl Aillinn
Rode from the country of her kin,
And old and young men rode with her:
For all that country had been astir
If anybody half as fair

Had chosen a husband anywhere
But where it could see her every day.
When they had ridden a little way
An old man caught the horse's head
With: "You must home again, and wed
With somebody in your own land."
A young man cried and kissed her hand,
"O lady, wed with one of us";
And when no face grew piteous
For any gentle thing she spake,
She fell and died of the heart-break.'
Because a lover's heart's worn out,
Being tumbled and blown about
By its own blind imagining,
And will believe that anything
That is bad enough to be true, is true,
Baile's heart was broken in two;
And he being laid upon green boughs,
Was carried to the goodly house
Where the Hound of Ulad sat before
The brazen pillars of his door,
His face bowed low to weep the end
Of the harper's daughter and her friend.
For although years had passed away
He always wept them on that day,
For on that day they had been betrayed;
And now that Honey-Mouth is laid
Under a cairn of sleepy stone
Before his eyes, he has tears for none,

Although he is carrying stone, but two
For whom the cairn's but heaped anew.
We hold because our memory is
So full of that thing and of this
That out of sight is out of mind.
But the grey rush under the wind
And the grey bird with crooked bill
Have such long memories, that they still
Remember Deirdre and her man;
And when we walk with Kate or Nan
About the windy water side,
Our heart can hear the voices chide.
How could we be so soon content,
Who know the way that Naoise went?
And they have news of Deirdre's eyes,
Who being lovely was so wise—
Ah! wise, my heart knows well how wise.
Now had that old gaunt crafty one,
Gathering his cloak about him, run
Where Aillinn rode with waiting maids,
Who amid leafy lights and shades
Dreamed of the hands that would unlace
Their bodices in some dim place
When they had come to the marriage bed;
And harpers, pondering with bowed head
A music that had thought enough
Of the ebb of all things to make love
Grow gentle without sorrowings;
And leather-coated men with slings

Who peered about on every side;
And amid leafy light he cried:
'He is well out of wind and wave;
They have heaped the stones above his grave
In Muirthemne, and over it
In changeless Ogham letters writ—
Baile, that was of Rury's seed.
'But the gods long ago decreed
No waiting maid should ever spread
Baile and Aillinn's marriage bed,
For they should clip and clip again
Where wild bees hive on the Great Plain.
Therefore it is but little news
That put this hurry in my shoes.'
And hurrying to the south, he came
To that high hill the herdsmen name
The Hill Seat of Leighin, because
Some god or king had made the laws
That held the land together there,
In old times among the clouds of the air.
That old man climbed; the day grew dim;
Two swans came flying up to him,
Linked by a gold chain each to each,
And with low murmuring laughing speech
Alighted on the windy grass.
They knew him: his changed body was
Tall, proud and ruddy, and light wings
Were hovering over the harp-strings
That Etain, Midhir's wife, had wove

In the hid place, being crazed by love.
What shall I call them? fish that swim,
Scale rubbing scale where light is dim
By a broad water-lily leaf;
Or mice in the one wheaten sheaf
Forgotten at the threshing place;
Or birds lost in the one clear space
Of morning light in a dim sky;
Or, it may be, the eyelids of one eye,
Or the door pillars of one house,
Or two sweet blossoming apple-boughs
That have one shadow on the ground;
Or the two strings that made one sound
Where that wise harper's finger ran.
For this young girl and this young man
Have happiness without an end,
Because they have made so good a friend.
They know all wonders, for they pass
The towery gates of Gorias,
And Findrias and Falias,
And long-forgotten Murias,
Among the giant kings whose hoard,
Cauldron and spear and stone and sword,
Was robbed before earth gave the wheat;
Wandering from broken street to street
They come where some huge watcher is,
And tremble with their love and kiss.
They know undying things, for they
Wander where earth withers away,

Though nothing troubles the great streams
But light from the pale stars, and gleams
From the holy orchards, where there is none
But fruit that is of precious stone,
Or apples of the sun and moon.
What were our praise to them? they eat
Quiet's wild heart, like daily meat;
Who when night thickens are afloat
On dappled skins in a glass boat,
Far out under a windless sky;
While over them birds of Aengus fly,
And over the tiller and the prow,
And waving white wings to and fro
Awaken wanderings of light air
To stir their coverlet and their hair.
And poets found, old writers say,
A yew tree where his body lay;
But a wild apple hid the grass
With its sweet blossom where hers was;
And being in good heart, because
A better time had come again
After the deaths of many men,
And that long fighting at the ford,
They wrote on tablets of thin board,
Made of the apple and the yew,
All the love stories that they knew.
Let rush and bird cry out their fill
Of the harper's daughter if they will,
Beloved, I am not afraid of her.

She is not wiser nor lovelier,
And you are more high of heart than she,
For all her wanderings over-sea;
But I'd have bird and rush forget
Those other two; for never yet
Has lover lived, but longed to wive
Like them that are no more alive.

[62]

[63]

[64]

[65]

IN THE SEVEN WOODS

I HAVE heard the pigeons of the Seven Woods
Make their faint thunder, and the garden bees
Hum in the lime tree flowers; and put away
The unavailing outcries and the old bitterness
That empty the heart. I have forgot awhile
Tara uprooted, and new commonness
Upon the throne and crying about the streets
And hanging its paper flowers from post to post,
Because it is alone of all things happy.
I am contented for I know that Quiet
Wanders laughing and eating her wild heart
Among pigeons and bees, while that Great Archer,
Who but awaits His hour to shoot, still hangs
A cloudy quiver over Parc-na-Lee.
AUGUST, 1902.

THE ARROW

I THOUGHT of your beauty, and this arrow,
Made out of a wild thought, is in my marrow.
There's no man may look upon her, no man;
As when newly grown to be a woman,
Blossom pale, she pulled down the pale blossom
At the moth hour and hid it in her bosom.
This beauty's kinder, yet for a reason
I could weep that the old is out of season.

THE FOLLY OF BEING COMFORTED

ONE that is ever kind said yesterday:

'Your well-beloved's hair has threads of grey,
And little shadows come about her eyes;
Time can but make it easier to be wise,
Though now it's hard, till trouble is at an end;
And so be patient, be wise and patient, friend.'
But, heart, there is no comfort, not a grain;
Time can but make her beauty over again,
Because of that great nobleness of hers;
The fire that stirs about her, when she stirs
Burns but more clearly. O she had not these ways,
When all the wild summer was in her gaze.
O heart! O heart! if she'd but turn her head,
You'd know the folly of being comforted.

OLD MEMORY

I THOUGHT to fly to her when the end of day
Awakens an old memory, and say,
'Your strength, that is so lofty and fierce and kind,
It might call up a new age, calling to mind
The queens that were imagined long ago,
Is but half yours: he kneaded in the dough
Through the long years of youth, and who would have thought
It all, and more than it all, would come to naught,
And that dear words meant nothing?' But enough,
For when we have blamed the wind we can blame love;
Or, if there needs be more, be nothing said
That would be harsh for children that have strayed.

NEVER GIVE ALL THE HEART

NEVER give all the heart, for love

Will hardly seem worth thinking of
To passionate women if it seem
Certain, and they never dream
That it fades out from kiss to kiss;
For everything that's lovely is
But a brief dreamy kind delight.
O never give the heart outright,
For they, for all smooth lips can say,
Have given their hearts up to the play.
And who could play it well enough
If deaf and dumb and blind with love?
He that made this knows all the cost,
For he gave all his heart and lost.

THE WITHERING OF THE BOUGHS

I CRIED when the moon was murmuring to the birds,
'Let peewit call and curlew cry where they will,
I long for your merry and tender and pitiful words,
For the roads are unending, and there is no place to my mind.'
The honey-pale moon lay low on the sleepy hill,
And I fell asleep upon lonely Echtge of streams.
No boughs have withered because of the wintry wind;
The boughs have withered because I have told them my dreams.
I know of the leafy paths that the witches take,
Who come with their crowns of pearl and their spindles of wool,
And their secret smile, out of the depths of the lake;
I know where a dim moon drifts, where the Danaan kind
Wind and unwind their dances when the light grows cool
On the island lawns, their feet where the pale foam gleams.
No boughs have withered because of the wintry wind;

The boughs have withered because I have told them my dreams.

I know of the sleepy country, where swans fly round

Coupled with golden chains, and sing as they fly.

A king and a queen are wandering there, and the sound

Has made them so happy and hopeless, so deaf and so blind

With wisdom, they wander till all the years have gone by;

I know, and the curlew and peewit on Echtge of streams.

No boughs have withered because of the wintry wind;

The boughs have withered because I have told them my dreams.

ADAM'S CURSE

WE sat together at one summer's end,

That beautiful mild woman, your close friend,

And you and I, and talked of poetry.

I said: 'A line will take us hours maybe;

Yet if it does not seem a moment's thought,

Our stitching and unstitching has been naught.

Better go down upon your marrow bones

And scrub a kitchen pavement, or break stones

Like an old pauper, in all kinds of weather;

For to articulate sweet sounds together

Is to work harder than all these, and yet

Be thought an idler by the noisy set

Of bankers, schoolmasters, and clergymen

The martyrs call the world.'

                        That woman then

Murmured with her young voice, for whose mild sake

There's many a one shall find out all heartache

In finding that it's young and mild and low:

'There is one thing that all we women know,

Although we never heard of it at school—
That we must labour to be beautiful.'
I said: 'It's certain there is no fine thing
Since Adam's fall but needs much labouring.
There have been lovers who thought love should be
So much compounded of high courtesy
That they would sigh and quote with learned looks
Precedents out of beautiful old books;
Yet now it seems an idle trade enough.'
We sat grown quiet at the name of love;
We saw the last embers of daylight die,
And in the trembling blue-green of the sky
A moon, worn as if it had been a shell
Washed by time's waters as they rose and fell
About the stars and broke in days and years. I
had a thought for no one's but your ears;
That you were beautiful, and that I strove
To love you in the old high way of love;
That it had all seemed happy, and yet we'd grown
As weary hearted as that hollow moon.

RED HANRAHAN'S SONG ABOUT IRELAND

THE old brown thorn trees break in two high over Cummen Strand,
Under a bitter black wind that blows from the left hand;
Our courage breaks like an old tree in a black wind and dies,
But we have hidden in our hearts the flame out of the eyes
Of Cathleen, the daughter of Houlihan.
The wind has bundled up the clouds high over Knocknarea,
And thrown the thunder on the stones for all that Maeve can say.
Angers that are like noisy clouds have set our hearts abeat;

But we have all bent low and low and kissed the quiet feet

Of Cathleen, the daughter of Houlihan.

The yellow pool has overflowed high up on Clooth-na-Bare,

For the wet winds are blowing out of the clinging air;

Like heavy flooded waters our bodies and our blood;

But purer than a tall candle before the Holy Rood

Is Cathleen, the daughter of Houlihan.

THE OLD MEN ADMIRING THEMSELVES IN THE WATER

I HEARD the old, old men say,

'Everything alters,

And one by one we drop away.'

They had hands like claws, and their knees

Were twisted like the old thorn trees

By the waters.

I heard the old, old men say,

'All that's beautiful drifts away

Like the waters.'

UNDER THE MOON

I HAVE no happiness in dreaming of Brycelinde,

Nor Avalon the grass-green hollow, nor Joyous Isle,

Where one found Lancelot crazed and hid him for a while;

Nor Ulad, when Naoise had thrown a sail upon the wind,

Nor lands that seem too dim to be burdens on the heart;

Land-under-Wave, where out of the moon's light and the sun's

Seven old sisters wind the threads of the long-lived ones;

Land-of-the-Tower, where Aengus has thrown the gates apart,

And Wood-of-Wonders, where one kills an ox at dawn,

To find it when night falls laid on a golden bier:

Therein are many queens like Branwen and Guinivere;

And Niamh and Laban and Fand, who could change to an otter or fawn,

And the wood-woman, whose lover was changed to a blue-eyed hawk;

And whether I go in my dreams by woodland, or dun, or shore,

Or on the unpeopled waves with kings to pull at the oar,

I hear the harp-string praise them, or hear their mournful talk.

Because of a story I heard under the thin horn

Of the third moon, that hung between the night and the day,

To dream of women whose beauty was folded in dismay,

Even in an old story, is a burden not to be borne.

THE HOLLOW WOOD

O HURRY to the water amid the trees,

For there the tall deer and his leman sigh

When they have but looked upon their images,

O that none ever loved but you and I!

Or have you heard that sliding silver-shoed,

Pale silver-proud queen-woman of the sky,

When the sun looked out of his golden hood,

O that none ever loved but you and I!

O hurry to the hollow wood, for there

I will drive out the deer and moon and cry—

O my share of the world, O yellow hair,

No one has ever loved but you and I!

O DO NOT LOVE TOO LONG

SWEETHEART, do not love too long:

I loved long and long,

And grew to be out of fashion

Like an old song.

All through the years of our youth

Neither could have known

Their own thought from the other's,

We were so much at one.

But, O in a minute she changed—

O do not love too long,

Or you will grow out of fashion

Like an old song.

THE PLAYERS ASK FOR A BLESSING ON THE PSALTERIES AND ON THEMSELVES

oices together:

H<small>URRY</small> to bless the hands that play,

The mouths that speak, the notes and strings,

O masters of the glittering town!

O! lay the shrilly trumpet down,

Though drunken with the flags that sway

Over the ramparts and the towers,

And with the waving of your wings.

ice:

Maybe they linger by the way.

One gathers up his purple gown;

One leans and mutters by the wall—

He dreads the weight of mortal hours.

voice:

O no, O no! they hurry down

Like plovers that have heard the call.

oice:

O kinsmen of the Three in One,

O kinsmen bless the hands that play.
The notes they waken shall live on
When all this heavy history's done;
Our hands, our hands must ebb away.
oices together:
The proud and careless notes live on,
But bless our hands that ebb away.

THE HAPPY TOWNLAND

THERE's many a strong farmer
Whose heart would break in two,
If he could see the townland
That we are riding to;
Boughs have their fruit and blossom
At all times of the year;
Rivers are running over
With red beer and brown beer.
An old man plays the bagpipes
In a golden and silver wood;
Queens, their eyes blue like the ice,
Are dancing in a crowd.
The little fox he murmured,
'O what of the world's bane?'
The sun was laughing sweetly,
The moon plucked at my rein;
But the little red fox murmured,
'O do not pluck at his rein,
He is riding to the townland
That is the world's bane.'
When their hearts are so high

That they would come to blows,
They unhook their heavy swords
From golden and silver boughs;
But all that are killed in battle
Awaken to life again:
It is lucky that their story
Is not known among men.
For O, the strong farmers
That would let the spade lie,
Their hearts would be like a cup
That somebody had drunk dry.
The little fox he murmured,
'O what of the world's bane?'
The sun was laughing sweetly,
The moon plucked at my rein;
But the little red fox murmured,
'O do not pluck at his rein,
He is riding to the townland
That is the world's bane.'
Michael will unhook his trumpet
From a bough overhead,
And blow a little noise
When the supper has been spread.
Gabriel will come from the water
With a fish tail, and talk
Of wonders that have happened
On wet roads where men walk,
And lift up an old horn
Of hammered silver, and drink

Till he has fallen asleep
Upon the starry brink.
The little fox he murmured,
'O what of the world's bane?'
The sun was laughing sweetly,
The moon plucked at my rein;
But the little red fox murmured,
'O do not pluck at his rein,
He is riding to the townland
That is the world's bane.'

EARLY POEMS

I
BALLADS AND LYRICS

'The stars are threshed, and the souls are threshed from their husks.'

WILLIAM BLAKE.

T<small>O</small> A. E.

EARLY POEMS:
BALLADS AND LYRICS

TO SOME I HAVE TALKED WITH BY THE FIRE. A DEDICATION TO A VOLUME OF EARLY POEMS

W_{HILE} I wrought out these fitful Danaan rhymes,

My heart would brim with dreams about the times

When we bent down above the fading coals;

And talked of the dark folk, who live in souls

Of passionate men, like bats in the dead trees;

And of the wayward twilight companies,

Who sigh with mingled sorrow and content,

Because their blossoming dreams have never bent

Under the fruit of evil and of good;

And of the embattled flaming multitude

Who rise, wing above wing, flame above flame,

And, like a storm, cry the Ineffable Name,

And with the clashing of their sword blades make

A rapturous music, till the morning break,

And the white hush end all, but the loud beat

Of their long wings, the flash of their white feet.

THE SONG OF THE HAPPY SHEPHERD

T_{HE} woods of Arcady are dead,

And over is their antique joy;

Of old the world on dreaming fed;

Gray Truth is now her painted toy;

Yet still she turns her restless head:

But O, sick children of the world,

Of all the many changing things
In dreary dancing past us whirled,
To the cracked tune that Chronos sings,
Words alone are certain good.
Where are now the warring kings,
Word bemockers?—By the Rood
Where are now the warring kings?
An idle word is now their glory,
By the stammering schoolboy said,
Reading some entangled story:
The kings of the old time are fled.
The wandering earth herself may be
Only a sudden flaming word,
In clanging space a moment heard,
Troubling the endless reverie.
Then no wise worship dusty deeds,
Nor seek—for this is also sooth—
To hunger fiercely after truth,
Lest all thy toiling only breeds
New dreams, new dreams; there is no truth
Saving in thine own heart. Seek, then,
No learning from the starry men,
Who follow with the optic glass
The whirling ways of stars that pass;
Seek, then—for this is also sooth—
No word of theirs: the cold star-bane
Has cloven and rent their hearts in twain,
And dead is all their human truth.
Go, gather by the humming sea

Some twisted, echo-harbouring shell,
And to its lips thy story tell,
And they thy comforters will be,
Rewording in melodious guile
Thy fretful words a little while,
Till they shall singing fade in ruth,
And die a pearly brotherhood;
For words alone are certain good:
Sing, then, for this is also sooth.
I must be gone: there is a grave
Where daffodil and lily wave,
And I would please the hapless faun,
Buried under the sleepy ground,
With mirthful songs before the dawn.
His shouting days with mirth were crowned;
And still I dream he treads the lawn,
Walking ghostly in the dew,
Pierced by my glad singing through,
My songs of old earth's dreamy youth:
But ah! she dreams not now; dream thou!
For fair are poppies on the brow:
Dream, dream, for this is also sooth.

THE SAD SHEPHERD

THERE was a man whom Sorrow named his friend,
And he, of his high comrade Sorrow dreaming,
Went walking with slow steps along the gleaming
And humming sands, where windy surges wend:
And he called loudly to the stars to bend
From their pale thrones and comfort him, but they

Among themselves laugh on and sing alway:
And then the man whom Sorrow named his friend
Cried out, *Dim sea, hear my most piteous story!*
The sea swept on and cried her old cry still,
Rolling along in dreams from hill to hill;
He fled the persecution of her glory
And, in a far-off, gentle valley stopping,
Cried all his story to the dewdrops glistening,
But naught they heard, for they are always listening,
The dewdrops, for the sound of their own dropping.
And then the man whom Sorrow named his friend,
Sought once again the shore, and found a shell
And thought, *I will my heavy story tell*
Till my own words, re-echoing, shall send
Their sadness through a hollow, pearly heart;
And my own tale again for me shall sing,
And my own whispering words be comforting,
And lo! my ancient burden may depart.
Then he sang softly nigh the pearly rim;
But the sad dweller by the sea-ways lone
Changed all he sang to inarticulate moan
Among her wildering whirls, forgetting him.

THE CLOAK, THE BOAT, AND THE SHOES

'W<small>HAT</small> do you make so fair and bright?'
'I make the cloak of Sorrow:
O, lovely to see in all men's sight
Shall be the cloak of Sorrow,
In all men's sight.'
'What do you build with sails for flight?'

'I build a boat for Sorrow,

O, swift on the seas all day and night

Saileth the rover Sorrow,

All day and night.'

'What do you weave with wool so white?'

'I weave the shoes of Sorrow,

Soundless shall be the footfall light

In all men's ears of Sorrow,

Sudden and light.'

ANASHUYA AND VIJAYA

A little Indian temple in the Golden Age. Around it a garden; around that the forest. ANASHUYA, *the young priestess, kneeling within the temple.*

ANASHUYA.

S<small>END</small> peace on all the lands and flickering corn.—

O, may tranquillity walk by his elbow

When wandering in the forest, if he love

No other.—Hear, and may the indolent flocks

Be plentiful.—And if he love another,

May panthers end him.—Hear, and load our king

With wisdom hour by hour.—May we two stand,

When we are dead, beyond the setting suns,

A little from the other shades apart,

With mingling hair, and play upon one lute.

VIJAYA [*entering and throwing a lily at her*]

Hail! hail, my Anashuya.

ANASHUYA.

No: be still.

I, priestess of this temple, offer up

Prayers for the land.

VIJAYA.

I will wait here, Amrita.

ANASHUYA.

By mighty Brahma's ever rustling robe,
Who is Amrita? Sorrow of all sorrows!
Another fills your mind.

VIJAYA.

My mother's name.

ANASHUYA [*sings, coming out of the temple*]

A sad, sad thought went by me slowly:
Sigh, O you little stars! O, sigh and shake your blue apparel!
The sad, sad thought has gone from me now wholly:
Sing, O you little stars! O sing, and raise your rapturous carol
To mighty Brahma, who has made you many as the sands,
And laid you on the gates of evening with his quiet hands.

[*Sits down on the steps of the temple*]

Vijaya, I have brought my evening rice;
The sun has laid his chin on the gray wood,
Weary, with all his poppies gathered round him.

VIJAYA.

The hour when Kama, full of sleepy laughter,
Rises, and showers abroad his fragrant arrows,
Piercing the twilight with their murmuring barbs.

ANASHUYA.

See how the sacred old flamingoes come,
Painting with shadow all the marble steps:
Aged and wise, they seek their wonted perches
Within the temple, devious walking, made

62

To wander by their melancholy minds.

Yon tall one eyes my supper; swiftly chase him

Far, far away. I named him after you.

He is a famous fisher; hour by hour

He ruffles with his bill the minnowed streams.

Ah! there he snaps my rice. I told you so.

Now cuff him off. He's off! A kiss for you,

Because you saved my rice. Have you no thanks?

VIJAYA [sings]

Sing you of her, O first few stars,

Whom Brahma, touching with his finger, praises, for you hold

The van of wandering quiet; ere you be too calm and old,

Sing, turning in your cars,

Sing, till you raise your hands and sigh, and from your car heads peer,

With all your whirling hair, and drop tear upon azure tear.

ANASHUYA.

What know the pilots of the stars of tears?

VIJAYA.

Their faces are all worn, and in their eyes

Flashes the fire of sadness, for they see

The icicles that famish all the north,

Where men lie frozen in the glimmering snow;

And in the flaming forests cower the lion

And lioness, with all their whimpering cubs;

And, ever pacing on the verge of things, The

phantom, Beauty, in a mist of tears;

While we alone have round us woven woods,

And feel the softness of each other's hand,

Amrita, while—

ANASHUYA [*going away from him*].

Ah me, you love another,

[*Bursting into tears*]

And may some dreadful ill befall her quick!

VIJAYA.

I loved another; now I love no other.

Among the mouldering of ancient woods

You live, and on the village border she,

With her old father the blind wood-cutter;

I saw her standing in her door but now.

ANASHUYA.

Vijaya, swear to love her never more.

VIJAYA.

Ay, ay.

ANASHUYA.

Swear by the parents of the gods,

Dread oath, who dwell on sacred Himalay,

On the far Golden Peak; enormous shapes,

Who still were old when the great sea was young;

On their vast faces mystery and dreams;

Their hair along the mountains rolled and filled

From year to year by the unnumbered nests

Of aweless birds, and round their stirless feet

The joyous flocks of deer and antelope,

Who never hear the unforgiving hound.

Swear!

VIJAYA.

By the parents of the gods, I swear.

ANASHUYA [*sings*].

I have forgiven, O new star!

Maybe you have not heard of us, you have come forth so newly,

You hunter of the fields afar!

Ah, you will know my loved one by his hunter's arrows truly,

Shoot on him shafts of quietness, that he may ever keep

An inner laughter, and may kiss his hands to me in sleep.

Farewell, Vijaya. Nay, no word, no word;

I, priestess of this temple, offer up

Prayers for the land.

[VIJAYA goes]

         O Brahma, guard in sleep

The merry lambs and the complacent kine,

The flies below the leaves, and the young mice

In the tree roots, and all the sacred flocks

Of red flamingo; and my love, Vijaya;

And may no restless fay with fidget finger

Trouble his sleeping: give him dreams of me.

THE INDIAN UPON GOD

I PASSED along the water's edge below the humid trees,

My spirit rocked in evening light, the rushes round my knees,

My spirit rocked in sleep and sighs; and saw the moorfowl pace

All dripping on a grassy slope, and saw them cease to chase

Each other round in circles, and heard the eldest speak:

Who holds the world between His bill and made us strong or weak

Is an undying moorfowl, and He lives beyond the sky.

The rains are from His dripping wing, the moonbeams from his eye.

I passed a little further on and heard a lotus talk:

Who made the world and ruleth it, He hangeth on a stalk,

For I am in His image made, and all this tinkling tide

Is but a sliding drop of rain between His petals wide.

A little way within the gloom a roebuck raised his eyes

Brimful of starlight, and he said: *The Stamper of the Skies,*

He is a gentle roebuck; for how else, I pray, could He

Conceive a thing so sad and soft, a gentle thing like me?

I passed a little further on and heard a peacock say:

Who made the grass and made the worms and made my feathers gay,

He is a monstrous peacock, and He waveth all the night

His languid tail above us, lit with myriad spots of light.

THE INDIAN TO HIS LOVE

T<small>HE</small> island dreams under the dawn

And great boughs drop tranquillity;

The peahens dance on a smooth lawn,

A parrot sways upon a tree,

Raging at his own image in the enamelled sea.

Here we will moor our lonely ship

And wander ever with woven hands,

Murmuring softly lip to lip,

Along the grass, along the sands,

Murmuring how far away are the unquiet lands:

How we alone of mortals are

Hid under quiet boughs apart,

While our love grows an Indian star,

A meteor of the burning heart,

One with the tide that gleams, the wings that gleam and dart,

The heavy boughs, the burnished dove

That moans and sighs a hundred days:

How when we die our shades will rove,

When eve has hushed the feathered ways,

Dropping a vapoury footsole on the tide's drowsy blaze.

THE FALLING OF THE LEAVES

A<small>UTUMN</small> is over the long leaves that love us,
And over the mice in the barley sheaves;
Yellow the leaves of the rowan above us,
And yellow the wet wild-strawberry leaves.
The hour of the waning of love has beset us,
And weary and worn are our sad souls now;
Let us part, ere the season of passion forget us,
With a kiss and a tear on thy drooping brow.

EPHEMERA

'Y<small>OUR</small> eyes that once were never weary of mine
Are bowed in sorrow under their trembling lids,
Because our love is waning.'
                        And then she:
'Although our love is waning, let us stand
By the lone border of the lake once more,
Together in that hour of gentleness
When the poor tired child, Passion, falls asleep:
How far away the stars seem, and how far
Is our first kiss, and ah, how old my heart!'
Pensive they paced along the faded leaves,
While slowly he whose hand held hers replied:
'Passion has often worn our wandering hearts.'
The woods were round them, and the yellow leaves
Fell like faint meteors in the gloom, and once
A rabbit old and lame limped down the path;
Autumn was over him: and now they stood

On the lone border of the lake once more:
Turning, he saw that she had thrust dead leaves
Gathered in silence, dewy as her eyes,
In bosom and hair.

        'Ah, do not mourn,' he said,
'That we are tired, for other loves await us:
Hate on and love through unrepining hours;
Before us lies eternity; our souls
Are love, and a continual farewell.'

THE MADNESS OF KING GOLL

I SAT on cushioned otter skin:
My word was law from Ith to Emen,
And shook at Invar Amargin
The hearts of the world-troubling seamen,
And drove tumult and war away
From girl and boy and man and beast;
The fields grew fatter day by day, The
wild fowl of the air increased; And
every ancient Ollave said,
While he bent down his fading head,
'He drives away the Northern cold.'
They will not hush, the leaves a-flutter round me, the beech leaves old.
I sat and mused and drank sweet wine;
A herdsman came from inland valleys,
Crying, the pirates drove his swine
To fill their dark-beaked hollow galleys.
I called my battle-breaking men,
And my loud brazen battle-cars
From rolling vale and rivery glen;

And under the blinking of the stars

Fell on the pirates by the deep,

And hurled them in the gulph of sleep:

These hands won many a torque of gold.

They will not hush, the leaves a-flutter round me, the beech leaves old.

But slowly, as I shouting slew

And trampled in the bubbling mire,

In my most secret spirit grew

A whirling and a wandering fire:

I stood: keen stars above me shone,

Around me shone keen eyes of men:

I laughed aloud and hurried on

By rocky shore and rushy fen;

I laughed because birds fluttered by,

And starlight gleamed, and clouds flew high,

And rushes waved and waters rolled.

They will not hush, the leaves a-flutter round me, the beech leaves old.

And now I wander in the woods

When summer gluts the golden bees,

Or in autumnal solitudes

Arise the leopard-coloured trees;

Or when along the wintry strands

The cormorants shiver on their rocks;

I wander on, and wave my hands,

And sing, and shake my heavy locks.

The grey wolf knows me; by one ear

I lead along the woodland deer;

The hares run by me growing bold.

They will not hush, the leaves a-flutter round me, the beech leaves old.

I came upon a little town,

That slumbered in the harvest moon,

And passed a-tiptoe up and down,

Murmuring, to a fitful tune,

How I have followed, night and day,

A tramping of tremendous feet,

And saw where this old tympan lay,

Deserted on a doorway seat,

And bore it to the woods with me;

Of some unhuman misery

Our married voices wildly trolled.

They will not hush, the leaves a-flutter round me, the beech leaves old.

I sang how, when day's toil is done,

Orchil shakes out her long dark hair

That hides away the dying sun

And sheds faint odours through the air:

When my hand passed from wire to wire

It quenched, with sound like falling dew,

The whirling and the wandering fire;

But lift a mournful ulalu,

For the kind wires are torn and still,

And I must wander wood and hill

Through summer's heat and winter's cold.

They will not hush, the leaves a-flutter round me, the beech leaves old.

THE STOLEN CHILD

W<small>HERE</small> dips the rocky highland

Of Sleuth Wood in the lake,

There lies a leafy island

Where flapping herons wake

The drowsy water rats;

There we've hid our faery vats.

Full of berries,

And of reddest stolen cherries.

Come away, O human child!

To the waters and the wild

With a faery, hand in hand,

For the world's more full of weeping than you can understand.

Where the wave of moonlight glosses

The dim gray sands with light,

Far off by furthest Rosses

We foot it all the night,

Weaving olden dances,

Mingling hands and mingling glances

Till the moon has taken flight;

To and fro we leap

And chase the frothy bubbles,

While the world is full of troubles

And is anxious in its sleep.

Come away, O human child!

To the waters and the wild

With a faery, hand in hand,

For the world's more full of weeping than you can understand.

Where the wandering water gushes

From the hills above Glen-Car,

In pools among the rushes

That scarce could bathe a star,

We seek for slumbering trout,

And whispering in their ears

Give them unquiet dreams;

Leaning softly out

From ferns that drop their tears

Over the young streams.

Come away, O human child!

To the waters and the wild

With a faery, hand in hand,

For the world's more full of weeping than you can understand.

Away with us he's going,

The solemn-eyed:

He'll hear no more the lowing

Of the calves on the warm hillside;

Or the kettle on the hob

Sing peace into his breast,

Or see the brown mice bob

Round and round the oatmeal-chest.

For he comes, the human child,

To the waters and the wild

With a faery, hand in hand,

From a world more full of weeping than he can understand.

TO AN ISLE IN THE WATER

Sʜʏ one, shy one,

Shy one of my heart,

She moves in the firelight

Pensively apart.

She carries in the dishes,

And lays them in a row.

To an isle in the water

With her would I go.

She carries in the candles

And lights the curtained room,

Shy in the doorway

And shy in the gloom;

And shy as a rabbit,

Helpful and shy.

To an isle in the water

With her would I fly.

DOWN BY THE SALLEY GARDENS

Down by the salley gardens my love and I did meet;

She passed the salley gardens with little snow-white feet.

She bid me take love easy, as the leaves grow on the tree;

But I, being young and foolish, with her would not agree.

In a field by the river my love and I did stand,

And on my leaning shoulder she laid her snow-white hand.

She bid me take life easy, as the grass grows on the weirs;

But I was young and foolish, and now am full of tears.

THE MEDITATION OF THE OLD FISHERMAN

You waves, though you dance by my feet like children at play,

Though you glow and you glance, though you purr and you dart;

In the Junes that were warmer than these are, the waves were more gay,

When I was a boy with never a crack in my heart.

The herring are not in the tides as they were of old;

My sorrow! for many a creak gave the creel in the cart

That carried the take to Sligo town to be sold,

When I was a boy with never a crack in my heart.

And ah, you proud maiden, you are not so fair when his oar

Is heard on the water, as they were, the proud and apart,

Who paced in the eve by the nets on the pebbly shore,
When I was a boy with never a crack in my heart.

THE BALLAD OF FATHER O'HART

Good Father John O'Hart
In penal days rode out
To a shoneen who had free lands
And his own snipe and trout.

In trust took he John's lands;
Sleiveens were all his race;
And he gave them as dowers to his daughters,
And they married beyond their place.

But Father John went up,
And Father John went down;
And he wore small holes in his shoes,
And he wore large holes in his gown.

All loved him, only the shoneen,
Whom the devils have by the hair,
From the wives, and the cats, and the children,
To the birds in the white of the air.

The birds, for he opened their cages
As he went up and down;
And he said with a smile, 'Have peace now';
And he went his way with a frown.

But if when any one died
Came keeners hoarser than rooks,
He bade them give over their keening;
For he was a man of books.

And these were the works of John,
When weeping score by score,

People came into Coloony;
For he'd died at ninety-four.
There was no human keening;
The birds from Knocknarea
And the world round Knocknashee
Came keening in that day.
The young birds and old birds
Came flying, heavy and sad;
Keening in from Tiraragh,
Keening from Ballinafad;
Keening from Inishmurray,
Nor stayed for bite or sup;
This way were all reproved
Who dig old customs up.

THE BALLAD OF MOLL MAGEE

COME round me, little childer;
There, don't fling stones at me
Because I mutter as I go;
But pity Moll Magee.
My man was a poor fisher
With shore lines in the say;
My work was saltin'herrings
The whole of the long day.
And sometimes from the saltin' shed,
I scarce could drag my feet
Under the blessed moonlight,
Along the pebbly street.
I'd always been but weakly,
And my baby was just born;

A neighbour minded her by day,
I minded her till morn.
I lay upon my baby;
Ye little childer dear,
I looked on my cold baby
When the morn grew frosty and clear.
A weary woman sleeps so hard!
My man grew red and pale,
And gave me money, and bade me go
To my own place, Kinsale.
He drove me out and shut the door,
And gave his curse to me;
I went away in silence,
No neighbour could I see.
The windows and the doors were shut,
One star shone faint and green;
The little straws were turnin' round
Across the bare boreen.
I went away in silence:
Beyond old Martin's byre
I saw a kindly neighbour
Blowin' her mornin' fire.
She drew from me my story—
My money's all used up,
And still, with pityin', scornin' eye,
She gives me bite and sup.
She says my man will surely come,
And fetch me home agin;
But always, as I'm movin' round,

Without doors or within,
Pilin' the wood or pilin' the turf,
Or goin' to the well,
I'm thinkin' of my baby
And keenin' to mysel'.
And sometimes I am sure she knows
When, openin' wide His door,
God lights the stars, His candles,
And looks upon the poor.
So now, ye little childer,
Ye won't fling stones at me;
But gather with your shinin' looks
And pity Moll Magee.

THE BALLAD OF THE FOXHUNTER

'Now lay me in a cushioned chair
And carry me, you four,
With cushions here and cushions there,
To see the world once more.
'And some one from the stables bring
My Dermot dear and brown,
And lead him gently in a ring,
And gently up and down.
'Now leave the chair upon the grass:
Bring hound and huntsman here,
And I on this strange road will pass,
Filled full of ancient cheer.'
His eyelids droop, his head falls low,
His old eyes cloud with dreams;
The sun upon all things that grow

Pours round in sleepy streams.
Brown Dermot treads upon the lawn,
And to the armchair goes,
And now the old man's dreams are gone,
He smooths the long brown nose.
And now moves many a pleasant tongue
Upon his wasted hands,
For leading aged hounds and young
The huntsman near him stands.
'My huntsman, Rody, blow the horn,
And make the hills reply.'
The huntsman loosens on the morn
A gay and wandering cry.
A fire is in the old man's eyes,
His fingers move and sway,
And when the wandering music dies
They hear him feebly say,
'My huntsman, Rody, blow the horn,
And make the hills reply.'
'I cannot blow upon my horn,
I can but weep and sigh.'
The servants round his cushioned place
Are with new sorrow wrung;
And hounds are gazing on his face,
Both aged hounds and young.
One blind hound only lies apart
On the sun-smitten grass;
He holds deep commune with his heart:
The moments pass and pass;

The blind hound with a mournful din

Lifts slow his wintry head;

The servants bear the body in;

The hounds wail for the dead.

THE BALLAD OF FATHER GILLIGAN

THE old priest Peter Gilligan
Was weary night and day;
For half his flock were in their beds,
Or under green sods lay.
Once, while he nodded on a chair,
At the moth-hour of eve,
Another poor man sent for him,
And he began to grieve.
'I have no rest, nor joy, nor peace,
For people die and die';
And after cried he, 'God forgive!
My body spake, not I!'
He knelt, and leaning on the chair
He prayed and fell asleep;
And the moth-hour went from the fields,
And stars began to peep.
They slowly into millions grew,
And leaves shook in the wind;
And God covered the world with shade,
And whispered to mankind.
Upon the time of sparrow chirp
When the moths came once more,
The old priest Peter Gilligan
Stood upright on the floor.
'Mavrone, mavrone! the man has died,
While I slept on the chair';
He roused his horse out of its sleep,
And rode with little care.
He rode now as he never rode,

By rocky lane and fen;

The sick man's wife opened the door:

'Father! you come again!'

'And is the poor man dead?' he cried.

'He died an hour ago.'

The old priest Peter Gilligan

In grief swayed to and fro.

'When you were gone, he turned and died

As merry as a bird.'

The old priest Peter Gilligan

He knelt him at that word.

'He who hath made the night of stars

For souls, who tire and bleed,

Sent one of His great angels down

To help me in my need.

'He who is wrapped in purple robes,

With planets in His care,

Had pity on the least of things

Asleep upon a chair.'

THE LAMENTATION OF THE OLD PENSIONER

I HAD a chair at every hearth,

When no one turned to see,

With 'Look at that old fellow there,

And who may he be?'

And therefore do I wander now,

And the fret lies on me.

The road-side trees keep murmuring:

Ah, wherefore murmur ye,

As in the old days long gone by,

Green oak and poplar tree?

The well-known faces are all gone

And the fret lies on me.

THE FIDDLER OF DOONEY

W_{HEN} I play on my fiddle in Dooney,

Folk dance like a wave of the sea;

My cousin is priest in Kilvarnet,

My brother in Moharabuiee.

I passed my brother and cousin:

They read in their books of prayer;

I read in my book of songs

I bought at the Sligo fair.

When we come at the end of time,

To Peter sitting in state,

He will smile on the three old spirits,

But call me first through the gate;

For the good are always the merry,

Save by an evil chance,

And the merry love the fiddle

And the merry love to dance:

And when the folk there spy me,

They will all come up to me,

With 'Here is the fiddler of Dooney!'

And dance like a wave of the sea.

THE DEDICATION TO A BOOK OF STORIES SELECTED FROM THE IRISH NOVELISTS

T_{HERE} was a green branch hung with many a bell

When her own people ruled in wave-worn Eire;

And from its murmuring greenness, calm of faery,

A Druid kindness, on all hearers fell.

It charmed away the merchant from his guile,

And turned the farmer's memory from his cattle,

And hushed in sleep the roaring ranks of battle,

For all who heard it dreamed a little while.

Ah, Exiles, wandering over many seas,

Spinning at all times Eire's good to-morrow!

Ah, worldwide Nation, always growing Sorrow!

I also bear a bell branch full of ease.

I tore it from green boughs winds tossed and hurled,

Green boughs of tossing always, weary, weary!

I tore it from the green boughs of old Eire,

The willow of the many-sorrowed world.

Ah, Exiles, wandering over many lands!

My bell branch murmurs: the gay bells bring laughter,

Leaping to shake a cobweb from the rafter;

The sad bells bow the forehead on the hands.

A honeyed ringing: under the new skies

They bring you memories of old village faces;

Cabins gone now, old well-sides, old dear places;

And men who loved the cause that never dies.

---

[134]
[135]

EARLY POEMS

II
THE ROSE

'Sero te amavi, Pulchritudo tam antiqua et tam nova! Sero te amavi.'

S. AUGUSTINE.

[137]
[138]

To Lionel Johnson

EARLY POEMS: THE ROSE

TO THE ROSE UPON THE ROOD OF TIME

Red Rose, proud Rose, sad Rose of all my days!
Come near me, while I sing the ancient ways:
Cuchulain battling with the bitter tide;
The Druid, gray, wood-nurtured, quiet-eyed,
Who cast round Fergus dreams, and ruin untold;
And thine own sadness, whereof stars, grown old
In dancing silver-sandalled on the sea,
Sing in their high and lonely melody.
Come near, that no more blinded by man's fate,
I find under the boughs of love and hate,
In all poor foolish things that live a day,
Eternal beauty wandering on her way.
Come near, come near, come near—Ah, leave me still
A little space for the rose-breath to fill!
Lest I no more hear common things that crave;
The weak worm hiding down in its small cave,
The field mouse running by me in the grass,
And heavy mortal hopes that toil and pass;
But seek alone to hear the strange things said
By God to the bright hearts of those long dead,
And learn to chaunt a tongue men do not know.
Come near; I would, before my time to go,
Sing of old Eire and the ancient ways:
Red Rose, proud Rose, sad Rose of all my days.

FERGUS AND THE DRUID

FERGUS.

THE whole day have I followed in the rocks,

And you have changed and flowed from shape to shape.

First as a raven on whose ancient wings

Scarcely a feather lingered, then you seemed

A weasel moving on from stone to stone,

And now at last you wear a human shape,

A thin gray man half lost in gathering night.

DRUID.

What would you, king of the proud Red Branch kings?

FERGUS.

This would I say, most wise of living souls:

Young subtle Conchubar sat close by me

When I gave judgment, and his words were wise,

And what to me was burden without end

To him seemed easy, so I laid the crown

Upon his head to cast away my care.

DRUID.

What would you, king of the proud Red Branch kings?

FERGUS.

I feast amid my people on the hill,

And pace the woods, and drive my chariot wheels

In the white border of the murmuring sea;

And still I feel the crown upon my head.

DRUID.

What would you, king of the proud Red Branch kings?

FERGUS.

I'd put away the foolish might of a king,

But learn the dreaming wisdom that is yours.

DRUID.

Look on my thin gray hair and hollow cheeks,
And on these hands that may not lift the sword,
This body trembling like a wind-blown reed.
No maiden loves me, no man seeks my help,
Because I be not of the things I dream.

FERGUS.

A wild and foolish labourer is a king,
To do and do and do, and never dream.

DRUID.

Take, if you must, this little bag of dreams;
Unloose the cord, and they will wrap you round.

FERGUS.

I see my life go dripping like a stream
From change to change; I have been many things,
A green drop in the surge, a gleam of light
Upon a sword, a fir-tree on a hill,
An old slave grinding at a heavy quern,
A king sitting upon a chair of gold,
And all these things were wonderful and great;
But now I have grown nothing, being all,
And the whole world weighs down upon my heart:
Ah! Druid, Druid, how great webs of sorrow
Lay hidden in the small slate-coloured thing!

THE DEATH OF CUCHULAIN

A MAN came slowly from the setting sun,
To Forgail's daughter, Emer, in her dun,
And found her dyeing cloth with subtle care,

And said, casting aside his draggled hair:
'I am Aleel, the swineherd, whom you bid
Go dwell upon the sea cliffs, vapour-hid;
But now my years of watching are no more.'
Then Emer cast the web upon the floor,
And stretching out her arms, red with the dye,
Parted her lips with a loud sudden cry.
Looking on her, Aleel, the swineherd, said:
'Not any god alive, nor mortal dead,
Has slain so mighty armies, so great kings,
Nor won the gold that now Cuchulain brings.'
'Why do you tremble thus from feet to crown?'
Aleel, the swineherd, wept and cast him down
Upon the web-heaped floor, and thus his word:
'With him is one sweet-throated like a bird,
And lovelier than the moon upon the sea;
He made for her an army cease to be.'
'Who bade you tell these things?' and then she cried
To those about, 'Beat him with thongs of hide
And drive him from the door.' And thus it was;
And where her son, Finmole, on the smooth grass
Was driving cattle, came she with swift feet,
And called out to him, 'Son, it is not meet
That you stay idling here with flocks and herds.'
'I have long waited, mother, for those words;
But wherefore now?'
                              'There is a man to die;
You have the heaviest arm under the sky.'
'My father dwells among the sea-worn bands,

And breaks the ridge of battle with his hands.'
'Nay, you are taller than Cuchulain, son.'
'He is the mightiest man in ship or dun.'
'Nay, he is old and sad with many wars,
And weary of the crash of battle cars.'
'I only ask what way my journey lies,
For God, who made you bitter, made you wise.'
'The Red Branch kings a tireless banquet keep,
Where the sun falls into the Western deep.
Go there, and dwell on the green forest rim;
But tell alone your name and house to him
Whose blade compels, and bid them send you one
Who has a like vow from their triple dun.'
Between the lavish shelter of a wood
And the gray tide, the Red Branch multitude
Feasted, and with them old Cuchulain dwelt,
And his young dear one close beside him knelt,
And gazed upon the wisdom of his eyes,
More mournful than the depth of starry skies,
And pondered on the wonder of his days;
And all around the harp-string told his praise,
And Conchubar, the Red Branch king of kings,
With his own fingers touched the brazen strings.
At last Cuchulain spake, 'A young man strays
Driving the deer along the woody ways.
I often hear him singing to and fro;
I often hear the sweet sound of his bow,
Seek out what man he is.'

                    One went and came.

'He bade me let all know he gives his name
At the sword point, and bade me bring him one
Who had a like vow from our triple dun.'
'I only of the Red Branch hosted now,'
Cuchulain cried, 'have made and keep that vow.'
After short fighting in the leafy shade,
He spake to the young man, 'Is there no maid
Who loves you, no white arms to wrap you round,
Or do you long for the dim sleepy ground,
That you come here to meet this ancient sword?'
'The dooms of men are in God's hidden hoard.'
'Your head a while seemed like a woman's head
That I loved once.'

                    Again the fighting sped,
But now the war rage in Cuchulain woke,
And through the other's shield his long blade broke,
And pierced him.

           'Speak before your breath is done.'
'I am Finmole, mighty Cuchulain's son.'
'I put you from your pain. I can no more.'
While day its burden on to evening bore,
With head bowed on his knees Cuchulain stayed;
Then Conchubar sent that sweet-throated maid,
And she, to win him, his gray hair caressed;
In vain her arms, in vain her soft white breast.
Then Conchubar, the subtlest of all men,
Ranking his Druids round him ten by ten,
Spake thus, 'Cuchulain will dwell there and brood
For three days more in dreadful quietude,

And then arise, and raving slay us all.
Go, cast on him delusions magical,
That he may fight the waves of the loud sea.'
And ten by ten under a quicken tree,
The Druids chaunted, swaying in their hands
Tall wands of alder and white quicken wands.
In three days' time, Cuchulain with a moan
Stood up, and came to the long sands alone:
For four days warred he with the bitter tide;
And the waves flowed above him, and he died.

THE ROSE OF THE WORLD

W<small>HO</small> dreamed that beauty passes like a dream?
For these red lips, with all their mournful pride,
Mournful that no new wonder may betide,
Troy passed away in one high funeral gleam,
And Usna's children died.

We and the labouring world are passing by:
Amid men's souls, that waver and give place,
Like the pale waters in their wintry race,
Under the passing stars, foam of the sky,
Lives on this lonely face.

Bow down, archangels, in your dim abode:
Before you were, or any hearts to beat,
Weary and kind one lingered by His seat;
He made the world to be a grassy road
Before her wandering feet.

THE ROSE OF PEACE

I<small>F</small> Michael, leader of God's host

When Heaven and Hell are met,
Looked down on you from Heaven's door-post
He would his deeds forget.
Brooding no more upon God's wars
In his Divine homestead,
He would go weave out of the stars
A chaplet for your head.
And all folk seeing him bow down,
And white stars tell your praise,
Would come at last to God's great town,
Led on by gentle ways;
And God would bid His warfare cease,
Saying all things were well;
And softly make a rosy peace,
A peace of Heaven with Hell.

THE ROSE OF BATTLE

Rose of all Roses, Rose of all the World!
The tall thought-woven sails, that flap unfurled
Above the tide of hours, trouble the air,
And God's bell buoyed to be the water's care;
While hushed from fear, or loud with hope, a band
With blown, spray-dabbled hair gather at hand.
Turn if you may from battles never done,
I call, as they go by me one by one,
Danger no refuge holds, and war no peace,
For him who hears love sing and never cease,
Beside her clean-swept hearth, her quiet shade:
But gather all for whom no love hath made
A woven silence, or but came to cast

A song into the air, and singing past
To smile on the pale dawn; and gather you
Who have sought more than is in rain or dew
Or in the sun and moon, or on the earth,
Or sighs amid the wandering, starry mirth,
Or comes in laughter from the sea's sad lips;
And wage God's battles in the long gray ships.
The sad, the lonely, the insatiable,
To these Old Night shall all her mystery tell;
God's bell has claimed them by the little cry
Of their sad hearts, that may not live nor die.

Rose of all Roses, Rose of all the World!

You, too, have come where the dim tides are hurled

Upon the wharves of sorrow, and heard ring

The bell that calls us on; the sweet far thing.

Beauty grown sad with its eternity

Made you of us, and of the dim gray sea.

Our long ships loose thought-woven sails and wait,

For God has bid them share an equal fate;

And when at last defeated in His wars,

They have gone down under the same white stars,

We shall no longer hear the little cry

Of our sad hearts, that may not live nor die.

A FAERY SONG

Sung by the people of faery over Diarmuid and Grania, who lay in their bridal sleep under a Cromlech.

W_E who are old, old and gay,

O so old!

Thousands of years, thousands of years,

If all were told:

Give to these children, new from the world,

Silence and love;

And the long dew-dropping hours of the night,

And the stars above:

Give to these children, new from the world,

Rest far from men.

Is anything better, anything better?

Tell us it then:

Us who are old, old and gay,

O so old!

Thousands of years, thousands of years,

If all were told.

THE LAKE ISLE OF INNISFREE

I WILL arise and go now, and go to Innisfree,

And a small cabin build there, of clay and wattles made;

Nine bean rows will I have there, a hive for the honey bee,

And live alone in the bee-loud glade.

And I shall have some peace there, for peace comes dropping slow,

Dropping from the veils of the morning to where the cricket sings;

There midnight's all a glimmer, and noon a purple glow,

And evening full of the linnet's wings.

I will arise and go now, for always night and day

I hear lake water lapping with low sounds by the shore;

While I stand on the roadway, or on the pavements gray,

I hear it in the deep heart's core.

A CRADLE SONG

THE angels are stooping

Above your bed;
They weary of trooping
With the whimpering dead.
God's laughing in heaven
To see you so good;
The shining Seven
Are gay with His mood.
I kiss you and kiss you,
My pigeon, my own;
Ah, how I shall miss you
When you have grown.

THE SONG OF THE OLD MOTHER

I RISE in the dawn, and I kneel and blow
Till the seed of the fire flicker and glow;
And then I must scrub and bake and sweep
Till stars are beginning to blink and peep;
And the young lie long and dream in their bed
Of the matching of ribbons for bosom and head,
And their day goes over in idleness,
And they sigh if the wind but lift a tress:
While I must work because I am old,
And the seed of the fire gets feeble and cold.

THE PITY OF LOVE

A PITY beyond all telling
Is hid in the heart of love:
The folk who are buying and selling;
The clouds on their journey above;
The cold wet winds ever blowing;

And the shadowy hazel grove
Where mouse-gray waters are flowing
Threaten the head that I love.

THE SORROW OF LOVE

THE quarrel of the sparrows in the eaves,
The full round moon and the star-laden sky,
And the loud song of the ever-singing leaves,
Had hid away earth's old and weary cry.

And then you came with those red mournful lips,
And with you came the whole of the world's tears,
And all the trouble of her labouring ships,
And all the trouble of her myriad years.

And now the sparrows warring in the eaves,
The curd-pale moon, the white stars in the sky,
And the loud chaunting of the unquiet leaves,
Are shaken with earth's old and weary cry.

WHEN YOU ARE OLD

WHEN you are old and gray and full of sleep,
And nodding by the fire, take down this book,
And slowly read, and dream of the soft look
Your eyes had once, and of their shadows deep;

How many loved your moments of glad grace,
And loved your beauty with love false or true;
But one man loved the pilgrim soul in you,
And loved the sorrows of your changing face.

And bending down beside the glowing bars
Murmur, a little sadly, how love fled
And paced upon the mountains overhead

And hid his face amid a crowd of stars.

THE WHITE BIRDS

I WOULD that we were, my beloved, white birds on the foam of the sea!

We tire of the flame of the meteor, before it can fade and flee;

And the flame of the blue star of twilight, hung low on the rim of the sky,

Has awaked in our hearts, my beloved, a sadness that may not die.

A weariness comes from those dreamers, dew-dabbled, the lily and rose;

Ah, dream not of them, my beloved, the flame of the meteor that goes,

Or the flame of the blue star that lingers hung low in the fall of the dew:

For I would we were changed to white birds on the wandering foam: I and you!

I am haunted by numberless islands, and many a Danaan shore,

Where Time would surely forget us, and Sorrow come near us no more;

Soon far from the rose and the lily, and fret of the flames would we be,

Were we only white birds, my beloved, buoyed out on the foam of the sea!

A DREAM OF DEATH

I DREAMED that one had died in a strange place

Near no accustomed hand:

And they had nailed the boards above her face,

The peasants of that land,

And, wondering, planted by her solitude

A cypress and a yew:

I came, and wrote upon a cross of wood,

Man had no more to do:

She was more beautiful than thy first love,

This lady by the trees:

And gazed upon the mournful stars above,

And heard the mournful breeze.

A DREAM OF A BLESSED SPIRIT

ALL the heavy days are over;
Leave the body's coloured pride
Underneath the grass and clover,
With the feet laid side by side.

One with her are mirth and duty;
Bear the gold embroidered dress,
For she needs not her sad beauty,
To the scented oaken press.

Hers the kiss of Mother Mary,
The long hair is on her face;
Still she goes with footsteps wary,
Full of earth's old timid grace.

With white feet of angels seven
Her white feet go glimmering;
And above the deep of heaven,
Flame on flame and wing on wing.

THE MAN WHO DREAMED OF FAERYLAND

HE stood among a crowd at Drumahair;
His heart hung all upon a silken dress,
And he had known at last some tenderness,
Before earth made of him her sleepy care;
But when a man poured fish into a pile,
It seemed they raised their little silver heads,
And sang how day a Druid twilight sheds
Upon a dim, green, well-beloved isle, Where
people love beside star-laden seas; How
Time may never mar their faery vows Under
the woven roofs of quicken boughs:

The singing shook him out of his new ease.
He wandered by the sands of Lisadill;
His mind ran all on money cares and fears,
And he had known at last some prudent years
Before they heaped his grave under the hill;
But while he passed before a plashy place,
A lug-worm with its gray and muddy mouth
Sang how somewhere to north or west or south
There dwelt a gay, exulting, gentle race;
And how beneath those three times blessed skies
A Danaan fruitage makes a shower of moons,
And as it falls awakens leafy tunes:
And at that singing he was no more wise.
He mused beside the well of Scanavin,
He mused upon his mockers: without fail
His sudden vengeance were a country tale,
Now that deep earth has drunk his body in;
But one small knot-grass growing by the pool
Told where, ah, little, all-unneeded voice!
Old Silence bids a lonely folk rejoice,
And chaplet their calm brows with leafage cool;
And how, when fades the sea-strewn rose of day,
A gentle feeling wraps them like a fleece,
And all their trouble dies into its peace:
The tale drove his fine angry mood away.
He slept under the hill of Lugnagall;
And might have known at last unhaunted sleep
Under that cold and vapour-turbaned steep,
Now that old earth had taken man and all:

Were not the worms that spired about his bones
A-telling with their low and reedy cry,
Of how God leans His hands out of the sky,
To bless that isle with honey in His tones;
That none may feel the power of squall and wave,
And no one any leaf-crowned dancer miss
Until He burn up Nature with a kiss:
The man has found no comfort in the grave.

THE TWO TREES

BELOVED, gaze in thine own heart,
The holy tree is growing there;
From joy the holy branches start,
And all the trembling flowers they bear.
The changing colours of its fruit
Have dowered the stars with merry light;
The surety of its hidden root
Has planted quiet in the night;
The shaking of its leafy head
Has given the waves their melody,
And made my lips and music wed,
Murmuring a wizard song for thee.
There, through bewildered branches, go
Winged Loves borne on in gentle strife,
Tossing and tossing to and fro
The flaming circle of our life.
When looking on their shaken hair,
And dreaming how they dance and dart,
Thine eyes grow full of tender care:
Beloved, gaze in thine own heart.

Gaze no more in the bitter glass
The demons, with their subtle guile,
Lift up before us when they pass,
Or only gaze a little while;
For there a fatal image grows,
With broken boughs, and blackened leaves,
And roots half hidden under snows
Driven by a storm that ever grieves.
For all things turn to barrenness
In the dim glass the demons hold,
The glass of outer weariness,
Made when God slept in times of old.
There, through the broken branches, go
The ravens of unresting thought;
Peering and flying to and fro,
To see men's souls bartered and bought.
When they are heard upon the wind,
And when they shake their wings; alas!
Thy tender eyes grow all unkind:
Gaze no more in the bitter glass.

TO IRELAND IN THE COMING TIMES

Know, that I would accounted be
True brother of that company,
Who sang to sweeten Ireland's wrong,
Ballad and story, rann and song;
Nor be I any less of them,
Because the red-rose-bordered hem
Of her, whose history began
Before God made the angelic clan,

Trails all about the written page;
For in the world's first blossoming age
The light fall of her flying feet
Made Ireland's heart begin to beat;
And still the starry candles flare
To help her light foot here and there;
And still the thoughts of Ireland brood
Upon her holy quietude.
Nor may I less be counted one
With Davis, Mangan, Ferguson,
Because to him, who ponders well,
My rhymes more than their rhyming tell
Of the dim wisdoms old and deep,
That God gives unto man in sleep.
For the elemental beings go
About my table to and fro.
In flood and fire and clay and wind,
They huddle from man's pondering mind;
Yet he who treads in austere ways
May surely meet their ancient gaze.
Man ever journeys on with them
After the red-rose-bordered hem.
Ah, faeries, dancing under the moon,
A Druid land, a Druid tune!
While still I may, I write for you
The love I lived, the dream I knew.
From our birthday, until we die, Is
but the winking of an eye;
And we, our singing and our love,

The mariners of night above,
And all the wizard things that go
About my table to and fro,
Are passing on to where may be,
In truth's consuming ecstasy,
No place for love and dream at all;
For God goes by with white foot-fall.
I cast my heart into my rhymes,
That you, in the dim coming times,
May know how my heart went with them
After the red-rose-bordered hem.

EARLY POEMS

III
THE WANDERINGS OF OISIN

'Give me the world if Thou wilt, but grant me an asylum for my affections.'

TULKA.

To Edwin J. Ellis

[172]
[173]

BOOK I

[174]
[175]

THE WANDERINGS OF OISIN

S. PATRIC.

Yοu who are bent, and bald, and blind,
With a heavy heart and a wandering mind,
Have known three centuries, poets sing,
Of dalliance with a demon thing.

OISIN.

Sad to remember, sick with years,
The swift innumerable spears,
The horsemen with their floating hair,
And bowls of barley, honey, and wine,
And feet of maidens dancing in tune,
And the white body that lay by mine;
But the tale, though words be lighter than air,
Must live to be old like the wandering moon.
Caolte, and Conan, and Finn were there,
When we followed a deer with our baying hounds,
With Bran, Sgeolan, and Lomair,
And passing the Firbolgs' burial mounds,
Came to the cairn-heaped grassy hill
Where passionate Maeve is stony still;
And found on the dove-gray edge of the sea
A pearl-pale, high-born lady, who rode
On a horse with bridle of findrinny;
And like a sunset were her lips,
A stormy sunset on doomed ships;
A citron colour gloomed in her hair,
But down to her feet white vesture flowed,

And with the glimmering crimson glowed

Of many a figured embroidery;

And it was bound with a pearl-pale shell

That wavered like the summer streams,

As her soft bosom rose and fell.

S. PATRIC.

You are still wrecked among heathen dreams.

OISIN.

'Why do you wind no horn?' she said.

'And every hero droop his head?

The hornless deer is not more sad

That many a peaceful moment had,

More sleek than any granary mouse,

In his own leafy forest house

Among the waving fields of fern:

The hunting of heroes should be glad.'

'O pleasant maiden,' answered Finn,

'We think on Oscar's pencilled urn,

And on the heroes lying slain,

On Gavra's raven-covered plain;

But where are your noble kith and kin,

And into what country do you ride?'

'My father and my mother are

Aengus and Edain, and my name

Is Niamh, and my land where tide

And sleep drown sun and moon and star.'

'What dream came with you that you came

To this dim shore on foam-wet feet?

Did your companion wander away

117

From where the birds of Aengus wing?'
She said, with laughter tender and sweet:
'I have not yet, war-weary king,
Been spoken of with any one;
For love of Oisin foam-wet feet
Have borne me where the tempests blind
Your mortal shores till time is done!'
'How comes it, princess, that your mind
Among undying people has run
On this young man, Oisin, my son?'
'I loved no man, though kings besought
And many a man of lofty name,
Until the Danaan poets came,
Bringing me honeyed, wandering thought
Of noble Oisin and his fame,
Of battles broken by his hands,
Of stories builded by his words
That are like coloured Asian birds
At evening in their rainless lands.'
O Patric, by your brazen bell,
There was no limb of mine but fell
Into a desperate gulph of love!
'You only will I wed,' I cried,
'And I will make a thousand songs,
And set your name all names above,
And captives bound with leathern thongs
Shall kneel and praise you, one by one,
At evening in my western dun.'
'O Oisin, mount by me and ride

To shores by the wash of the tremulous tide,
Where men have heaped no burial mounds,
And the days pass by like a wayward tune,
Where broken faith has never been known,
And the blushes of first love never have flown;
And there I will give you a hundred hounds;
No mightier creatures bay at the moon;
And a hundred robes of murmuring silk,
And a hundred calves and a hundred sheep
Whose long wool whiter than sea froth flows,
And a hundred spears and a hundred bows,
And oil and wine and honey and milk,
And always never-anxious sleep;
While a hundred youths, mighty of limb,
But knowing nor tumult nor hate nor strife,
And a hundred maidens, merry as birds,
Who when they dance to a fitful measure
Have a speed like the speed of the salmon herds,
Shall follow your horn and obey your whim,
And you shall know the Danaan leisure:
And Niamh be with you for a wife.'
Then she sighed gently, 'It grows late,
Music and love and sleep await,
Where I would be when the white moon climbs,
The red sun falls, and the world grows dim.'
And then I mounted and she bound me
With her triumphing arms around me,
And whispering to herself enwound me;
But when the horse had felt my weight,

He shook himself and neighed three times:
Caolte, Conan, and Finn came near,
And wept, and raised their lamenting hands,
And bid me stay, with many a tear;
But we rode out from the human lands.
In what far kingdom do you go,
Ah, Fenians, with the shield and bow?
Or are you phantoms white as snow,
Whose lips had life's most prosperous glow?
O you, with whom in sloping valleys,
Or down the dewy forest alleys,
I chased at morn the flying deer,
With whom I hurled the hurrying spear,
And heard the foemen's bucklers rattle,
And broke the heaving ranks of battle!
And Bran, Sgeolan, and Lomair,
Where are you with your long rough hair?
You go not where the red deer feeds,
Nor tear the foemen from their steeds.

S. PATRIC.

Boast not, nor mourn with drooping head
Companions long accurst and dead,
And hounds for centuries dust and air.

OISIN.

We galloped over the glossy sea:
I know not if days passed or hours,
And Niamh sang continually
Danaan songs, and their dewy showers
Of pensive laughter, unhuman sound,

Lulled weariness, and softly round
My human sorrow her white arms wound.
On! on! and now a hornless deer
Passed by us, chased by a phantom hound
All pearly white, save one red ear;
And now a maiden rode like the wind
With an apple of gold in her tossing hand,
And with quenchless eyes and fluttering hair
A beautiful young man followed behind.
'Were these two born in the Danaan land,
Or have they breathed the mortal air?'
'Vex them no longer,' Niamh said,
And sighing bowed her gentle head,
And sighing laid the pearly tip
Of one long finger on my lip.
But now the moon like a white rose shone
In the pale west, and the sun's rim sank,
And clouds arrayed their rank on rank
About his fading crimson ball:
The floor of Emen's hosting hall
Was not more level than the sea,
As full of loving phantasy,
And with low murmurs we rode on,
Where many a trumpet-twisted shell
That in immortal silence sleeps
Dreaming of her own melting hues,
Her golds, her ambers, and her blues,
Pierced with soft light the shallowing deeps.
But now a wandering land breeze came

And a far sound of feathery quires;
It seemed to blow from the dying flame,
They seemed to sing in the smouldering fires.
The horse towards the music raced,
Neighing along the lifeless waste;
Like sooty fingers, many a tree
Rose ever out of the warm sea;
And they were trembling ceaselessly,
As though they all were beating time,
Upon the centre of the sun,
To that low laughing woodland rhyme.
And, now our wandering hours were done,
We cantered to the shore, and knew
The reason of the trembling trees:
Round every branch the song-birds flew,
Or clung thereon like swarming bees;
While round the shore a million stood
Like drops of frozen rainbow light,
And pondered in a soft vain mood,
Upon their shadows in the tide,
And told the purple deeps their pride,
And murmured snatches of delight;
And on the shores were many boats
With bending sterns and bending bows,
And carven figures on their prows
Of bitterns, and fish-eating stoats,
And swans with their exultant throats:
And where the wood and waters meet
We tied the horse in a leafy clump,

And Niamh blew three merry notes
Out of a little silver trump;
And then an answering whisper flew
Over the bare and woody land,
A whisper of impetuous feet,
And ever nearer, nearer grew;
And from the woods rushed out a band
Of men and maidens, hand in hand,
And singing, singing altogether;
Their brows were white as fragrant milk,
Their cloaks made out of yellow silk,
And trimmed with many a crimson feather:
And when they saw the cloak I wore
Was dim with mire of a mortal shore,
They fingered it and gazed on me
And laughed like murmurs of the sea;
But Niamh with a swift distress
Bid them away and hold their peace;
And when they heard her voice they ran
And knelt them, every maid and man,
And kissed, as they would never cease,
Her pearl-pale hand and the hem of her dress.
She bade them bring us to the hall
Where Aengus dreams, from sun to sun,
A Druid dream of the end of days
When the stars are to wane and the world be done.
They led us by long and shadowy ways
Where drops of dew in myriads fall,
And tangled creepers every hour

Blossom in some new crimson flower,
And once a sudden laughter sprang
From all their lips, and once they sang
Together, while the dark woods rang,
And made in all their distant parts,
With boom of bees in honey marts,
A rumour of delighted hearts.
And once a maiden by my side
Gave me a harp, and bid me sing,
And touch the laughing silver string;
But when I sang of human joy
A sorrow wrapped each merry face,
And, Patric! by your beard, they wept,
Until one came, a tearful boy;
'A sadder creature never stept
Than this strange human bard,' he cried;
And caught the silver harp away,
And, weeping over the white strings, hurled
It down in a leaf-hid hollow place
That kept dim waters from the sky;
And each one said with a long, long sigh,
'O saddest harp in all the world,
Sleep there till the moon and the stars die!'
And now still sad we came to where
A beautiful young man dreamed within
A house of wattles, clay, and skin;
One hand upheld his beardless chin,
And one a sceptre flashing out
Wild flames of red and gold and blue,

Like to a merry wandering rout
Of dancers leaping in the air;
And men and maidens knelt them there
And showed their eyes with teardrops dim,
And with low murmurs prayed to him,
And kissed the sceptre with red lips,
And touched it with their finger-tips.
He held that flashing sceptre up.
'Joy drowns the twilight in the dew,
And fills with stars night's purple cup,
And wakes the sluggard seeds of corn,
And stirs the young kid's budding horn,
And makes the infant ferns unwrap,
And for the peewit paints his cap,
And rolls along the unwieldy sun,
And makes the little planets run:
And if joy were not on the earth,
There were an end of change and birth,
And earth and heaven and hell would die,
And in some gloomy barrow lie
Folded like a frozen fly;
Then mock at Death and Time with glances
And waving arms and wandering dances.
'Men's hearts of old were drops of flame
That from the saffron morning came,
Or drops of silver joy that fell
Out of the moon's pale twisted shell;
But now hearts cry that hearts are slaves,
And toss and turn in narrow caves;

But here there is nor law nor rule,
Nor have hands held a weary tool;
And here there is nor Change nor Death,
But only kind and merry breath,
For joy is God and God is joy.'
With one long glance on maid and boy
And the pale blossom of the moon,
He fell into a Druid swoon.
And in a wild and sudden dance
We mocked at Time and Fate and Chance,
And swept out of the wattled hall
And came to where the dewdrops fall
Among the foamdrops of the sea,
And there we hushed the revelry;
And, gathering on our brows a frown,
Bent all our swaying bodies down,
And to the waves that glimmer by
That slooping green De Danaan sod
Sang, 'God is joy and joy is God,
And things that have grown sad are wicked,
And things that fear the dawn of the morrow,
Or the gray wandering osprey Sorrow.'
We danced to where in the winding thicket
The damask roses, bloom on bloom,
Like crimson meteors hang in the gloom,
And bending over them softly said,
Bending over them in the dance,
With a swift and friendly glance
From dewy eyes: 'Upon the dead

Fall the leaves of other roses,

On the dead dim earth encloses:

But never, never on our graves,

Heaped beside the glimmering waves,

Shall fall the leaves of damask roses.

For neither Death nor Change comes near us,

And all listless hours fear us,

And we fear no dawning morrow,

Nor the gray wandering osprey Sorrow.'

The dance wound through the windless woods;

The ever-summered solitudes;

Until the tossing arms grew still

Upon the woody central hill;

And, gathered in a panting band,

We flung on high each waving hand,

And sang unto the starry broods:

In our raised eyes there flashed aglow

Of milky brightness to and fro

As thus our song arose: 'You stars,

Across your wandering ruby cars

Shake the loose reins: you slaves of God,

He rules you with an iron rod,

He holds you with an iron bond,

Each one woven to the other,

Each one woven to his brother

Like bubbles in a frozen pond;

But we in a lonely land abide

Unchainable as the dim tide,

With hearts that know nor law nor rule,

And hands that hold no wearisome tool;
Folded in love that fears no morrow,
Nor the gray wandering osprey Sorrow.'
O Patric! for a hundred years
I chased upon that woody shore
The deer, the badger, and the boar.
O Patric! for a hundred years
At evening on the glimmering sands,
Beside the piled-up hunting spears,
These now outworn and withered hands
Wrestled among the island bands.
O Patric! for a hundred years
We went a-fishing in long boats
With bending sterns and bending bows,
And carven figures on their prows
Of bitterns and fish-eating stoats.
O Patric! for a hundred years
The gentle Niamh was my wife;
But now two things devour my life;
The things that most of all I hate:
Fasting and prayers.

S. PATRIC.

Tell on.

OISIN.

Yes, yes,
For these were ancient Oisin's fate
Loosed long ago from heaven's gate,
For his last days to lie in wait.
When one day by the shore I stood,

I drew out of the numberless
White flowers of the foam a staff of wood
From some dead warrior's broken lance:
I turned it in my hands; the stains
Of war were on it, and I wept,
Remembering how the Fenians stept
Along the blood-bedabbled plains,
Equal to good or grievous chance:
Thereon young Niamh softly came
And caught my hands, but spake no word
Save only many times my name,
In murmurs, like a frighted bird.
We passed by woods, and lawns of clover,
And found the horse and bridled him,
For we knew well the old was over.
I heard one say 'his eyes grow dim
With all the ancient sorrow of men';
And wrapped in dreams rode out again
With hoofs of the pale findrinny
Over the glimmering purple sea:
Under the golden evening light.
The immortals moved among the fountains
By rivers and the woods' old night;
Some danced like shadows on the mountains,
Some wandered ever hand in hand,
Or sat in dreams on the pale strand;
Each forehead like an obscure star
Bent down above each hooked knee:
And sang, and with a dreamy gaze

Watched where the sun in a saffron blaze

Was slumbering half in the sea ways;

And, as they sang, the painted birds

Kept time with their bright wings and feet;

Like drops of honey came their words,

But fainter than a young lamb's bleat.

'An old man stirs the fire to a blaze,

In the house of a child, of a friend, of a brother;

He has over-lingered his welcome; the days,

Grown desolate, whisper and sigh to each other;

He hears the storm in the chimney above,

And bends to the fire and shakes with the cold,

While his heart still dreams of battle and love,

And the cry of the hounds on the hills of old.

'But we are apart in the grassy places,

Where care cannot trouble the least of our days,

Or the softness of youth be gone from our faces,

Or love's first tenderness die in our gaze.

The hare grows old as she plays in the sun

And gazes around her with eyes of brightness;

Before the swift things that she dreamed of were done

She limps along in an aged whiteness;

A storm of birds in the Asian trees

Like tulips in the air a-winging,

And the gentle waves of the summer seas,

That raise their heads and wander singing,

Must murmur at last "unjust, unjust";

And "my speed is a weariness," falters the mouse;

And the kingfisher turns to a ball of dust,

And the roof falls in of his tunnelled house.
But the love-dew dims our eyes till the day
When God shall come from the sea with a sigh
And bid the stars drop down from the sky, And
the moon like a pale rose wither away.'

BOOK II

[194]
[195]

THE WANDERINGS OF OISIN

Now, man of croziers, shadows called our names
And then away, away, like whirling flames;
And now fled by, mist-covered, without sound,
The youth and lady and the deer and hound;
'Gaze no more on the phantoms,' Niamh said,
And kissed my eyes, and, swaying her bright head
And her bright body, sang of faery and man
Before God was or my old line began;
Wars shadowy, vast, exultant; faeries of old
Who wedded men with rings of Druid gold;
And how those lovers never turn their eyes
Upon the life that fades and flickers and dies,
But love and kiss on dim shores far away
Rolled round with music of the sighing spray:
But sang no more, as when, like a brown bee
That has drunk full, she crossed the misty sea
With me in her white arms a hundred years
Before this day; for now the fall of tears
Troubled her song.
             I do not know if days
Or hours passed by, yet hold the morning rays
Shone many times among the glimmering flowers
Wove in her flower-like hair, before dark towers
Rose in the darkness, and the white surf gleamed
About them; and the horse of faery screamed
And shivered, knowing the Isle of many Fears,
Nor ceased until white Niamh stroked his ears

And named him by sweet names.

                        A foaming tide
Whitened afar with surge, fan-formed and wide,
Burst from a great door marred by many a blow
From mace and sword and pole-axe, long ago
When gods and giants warred. We rode between
The seaweed-covered pillars, and the green
And surging phosphorus alone gave light
On our dark pathway, till a countless flight
Of moonlit steps glimmered; and left and right
Dark statues glimmered over the pale tide
Upon dark thrones. Between the lids of one
The imaged meteors had flashed and run
And had disported in the stilly jet,
And the fixed stars had dawned and shone and set,
Since God made Time and Death and Sleep: the other
Stretched his long arm to where, a misty smother,
The stream churned, churned, and churned—his lips apart,
As though he told his never slumbering heart
Of every foamdrop on its misty way:
Tying the horse to his vast foot that lay
Half in the unvesselled sea, we climbed the stairs
And climbed so long, I thought the last steps were
Hung from the morning star; when these mild words
Fanned the delighted air like wings of birds:
'My brothers spring out of their beds at morn,
A-murmur like young partridge: with loud horn
They chase the noon-tide deer;
And when the dew-drowned stars hang in the air

Look to long fishing-lines, or point and pare
A larch-wood hunting spear.
'O sigh, O fluttering sigh, be kind to me;
Flutter along the froth lips of the sea,
And shores the froth lips wet:
And stay a little while, and bid them weep:
Ah, touch their blue veined eyelids if they sleep,
And shake their coverlet.
'When you have told how I weep endlessly,
Flutter along the froth lips of the sea
And home to me again,
And in the shadow of my hair lie hid,
And tell me how you came to one unbid,
The saddest of all men.'
A maiden with soft eyes like funeral tapers,
And face that seemed wrought out of moonlit vapours,
And a sad mouth, that fear made tremulous
As any ruddy moth, looked down on us;
And she with a wave-rusted chain was tied
To two old eagles, full of ancient pride,
That with dim eyeballs stood on either side.
Few feathers were on their dishevelled wings,
For their dim minds were with the ancient things.
'I bring deliverance,' pearl-pale Niamh said.
'Neither the living, nor the unlabouring dead,
Nor the high gods who never lived, may fight
My enemy and hope; demons for fright
Jabber and scream about him in the night;
For he is strong and crafty as the seas

That sprang under the Seven Hazel Trees.
And I must needs endure and hate and weep,
Until the gods and demons drop asleep,
Hearing Aed touch the mournful strings of gold.'
'Is he so dreadful?'

                'Be not over-bold,
But flee while you may flee from him.'

                      Then I:
'This demon shall be pierced and drop and die,
And his loose bulk be thrown in the loud tide.'
'Flee from him,' pearl-pale Niamh weeping cried,
'For all men flee the demons'; but moved not,
Nor shook my firm and spacious soul one jot;
There was no mightier soul of Heber's line;
Now it is old and mouse-like: for a sign
I burst the chain: still earless, nerveless, blind,
Wrapped in the things of the unhuman mind,
In some dim memory or ancient mood
Still earless, nerveless, blind, the eagles stood.
And then we climbed the stair to a high door,
A hundred horsemen on the basalt floor
Beneath had paced content: we held our way
And stood within: clothed in a misty ray
I saw a foam-white seagull drift and float
Under the roof, and with a straining throat
Shouted, and hailed him: he hung there a star,
For no man's cry shall ever mount so far;
Not even your God could have thrown down that hall;
Stabling His unloosed lightnings in their stall,

He had sat down and sighed with cumbered heart,
As though His hour were come.

                   We sought the part
That was most distant from the door; green slime
Made the way slippery, and time on time
Showed prints of sea-born scales, while down through it
The captives' journeys to and fro were writ
Like a small river, and, where feet touched, came
A momentary gleam of phosphorus flame.
Under the deepest shadows of the hall
That maiden found a ring hung on the wall,
And in the ring a torch, and with its flare
Making a world about her in the air,
Passed under a dim doorway, out of sight,
And came again, holding a second light
Burning between her fingers, and in mine
Laid it and sighed: I held a sword whose shine
No centuries could dim: and a word ran
Thereon in Ogham letters, 'Mananan':
That sea-god's name, who in a deep content
Sprang dripping, and, with captive demons sent
Out of the seven-fold seas, built the dark hall
Rooted in foam and clouds, and cried to all
The mightier masters of a mightier race;
And at his cry there came no milk-pale face
Under a crown of thorns and dark with blood,
But only exultant faces.

                Niamh stood
With bowed head, trembling when the white blade shone,

But she whose hours of tenderness were gone
Had neither hope nor fear. I bade them hide
Under the shadows till the tumults died
Of the loud crashing and earth-shaking fight,
Lest they should look upon some dreadful sight;
And thrust the torch between the slimy flags.
A dome made out of endless carven jags,
Where shadowy face flowed into shadowy face,
Looked down on me; and in the self-same place
I waited hour by hour, and the high dome
Windowless, pillarless, multitudinous home
Of faces, waited; and the leisured gaze
Was loaded with the memory of days
Buried and mighty: when through the great door
The dawn came in, and glimmered on the floor
With a pale light, I journeyed round the hall
And found a door deep sunken in the wall,
The least of doors; beyond on a dim plain
A little runnel made a bubbling strain,
And on the runnel's stony and bare edge
A dusky demon dry as a withered sedge
Swayed, crooning to himself an unknown tongue:
In a sad revelry he sang and swung
Bacchant and mournful, passing to and fro
His hand along the runnel's side, as though
The flowers still grew there: far on the sea's waste;
Shaking and waving, vapour vapour chased,
While high frail cloudlets, fed with a green light,
Like drifts of leaves, immovable and bright,

Hung in the passionate dawn. He slowly turned:
A demon's leisure: eyes, first white, now burned
Like wings of kingfishers; and he arose
Barking. We trampled up and down with blows
Of sword and brazen battle-axe, while day
Gave to high noon and noon to night gave way;
But when at withering of the sun he knew
The Druid sword of Mananan, he grew
To many shapes; I lunged at the smooth throat
Of a great eel; it changed, and I but smote
A fir-tree roaring in its leafless top;
And I but held a corpse, with livid chop
And dripping and sunken shape, to face and breast,
When I tore down that tree; but when the west
Surged up in plumy fire, I lunged and drave
Through heart and spine, and cast him in the wave,
Lest Niamh shudder.
                    Full of hope and dread
Those two came carrying wine and meat and bread,
And healed my wounds with unguents out of flowers,
That feed white moths by some De Danaan shrine;
Then in that hall, lit by the dim sea-shine,
We lay on skins of otters, and drank wine,
Brewed by the sea-gods, from huge cups that lay
Upon the lips of sea-gods in their day;
And then on heaped-up skins of otters slept.
But when the sun once more in saffron stept,
Rolling his flagrant wheel out of the deep,
We sang the loves and angers without sleep,

And all the exultant labours of the strong:
But now the lying clerics murder song
With barren words and flatteries of the weak.
In what land do the powerless turn the beak
Of ravening Sorrow, or the hand of Wrath?
For all your croziers, they have left the path
And wander in the storms and clinging snows,
Hopeless for ever: ancient Oisin knows,
For he is weak and poor and blind, and lies
On the anvil of the world.

S. PATRIC.

Be still: the skies
Are choked with thunder, lightning, and fierce wind,
For God has heard, and speaks His angry mind;
Go cast your body on the stones and pray,
For He has wrought midnight and dawn and day.

OISIN.

Saint, do you weep? I hear amid the thunder
The Fenian horses; armour torn asunder;
Laughter and cries: the armies clash and shock;
All is done now; I see the ravens flock;
Ah, cease, you mournful, laughing Fenian horn!
We feasted for three days. On the fourth morn
I found, dropping sea-foam on the wide stair,
And hung with slime, and whispering in his hair,
That demon dull and unsubduable;
And once more to a day-long battle fell,
And at the sundown threw him in the surge,
To lie until the fourth morn saw emerge

His new healed shape: and for a hundred years
So warred, so feasted, with nor dreams, nor fears
Nor languor nor fatigue: an endless feast,
An endless war.

              The hundred years had ceased;
I stood upon the stair: the surges bore
A beech bough to me, and my heart grew sore,
Remembering how I stood by white-haired Finn
While the woodpecker made a merry din,
The hare leaped in the grass.

                    Young Niamh came
Holding that horse, and sadly called my name;
I mounted, and we passed over the lone
And drifting grayness, while this monotone,
Surly and distant, mixed inseparably
Into the clangour of the wind and sea:
'I hear my soul drop down into decay,
And Mananan's dark tower, stone by stone,
Gather sea-slime and fall the seaward way,
And the moon goad the waters night and day,
That all be overthrown.
'But till the moon has taken all, I wage
War on the mightiest men under the skies,
And they have fallen or fled, age after age:
Light is man's love, and lighter is man's rage;
His purpose drifts and dies.'
And then lost Niamh murmured, 'Love, we go
To the Island of Forgetfulness, for lo!
The Islands of Dancing and of Victories

Are empty of all power.'

                    'And which of these

Is the Island of Content?'

                    'None know,' she said;

And on my bosom laid her weeping head.

BOOK III

[208]
[209]

THE WANDERINGS OF OISIN

FLED foam underneath us, and round us, a wandering and milky smoke,

High as the saddle girth, covering away from our glances the tide;

And those that fled, and that followed, from the foam-pale distance broke;

The immortal desire of immortals we saw in their faces, and sighed.

I mused on the chase with the Fenians, and Bran, Sgeolan, Lomair,

And never a song sang Niamh, and over my finger-tips

Came now the sliding of tears and sweeping of mist-cold air,

And now the warmth of sighs, and after the quiver of lips.

Were we days long or hours long in riding, when rolled in a grisly peace,

An isle lay level before us, with dripping hazel and oak?

And we stood on a sea's edge we saw not; for whiter than new-washed fleece

Fled foam underneath us, and round us, a wandering and milky smoke.

And we rode on the plains of the sea's edge; the sea's edge barren and gray,

Gray sand on the green of the grasses and over the dripping trees,

Dripping and doubling landward, as though they would hasten away

Like an army of old men longing for rest from the moan of the seas.

But the trees grew taller and closer, immense in their wrinkling bark;

Dropping; a murmurous dropping; old silence and that one sound;

For no live creatures lived there, no weasels moved in the dark:

Long sighs arose in our spirits, beneath us bubbled the ground.

And the ears of the horse went sinking away in the hollow night,

For, as drift from a sailor slow drowning the gleams of the world and the sun,

Ceased on our hands and our faces, on hazel and oak leaf, the light,

And the stars were blotted above us, and the whole of the world was one.

Till the horse gave a whinny; for, cumbrous with stems of the hazel and oak,

A valley flowed down from his hoofs, and there in the long grass lay,

Under the starlight and shadow, a monstrous slumbering folk,

Their naked and gleaming bodies poured out and heaped in the way.

And by them were arrow and war-axe, arrow and shield and blade;

And dew-blanched horns, in whose hollow a child of three years old

Could sleep on a bed of rushes, and all inwrought and inlaid,

And more comely than man can make them with bronze and silver and gold.

And each of the huge white creatures was huger than four-score men;

The tops of their ears were feathered, their hands were the claws of birds,

And, shaking the plumes of the grasses and the leaves of the mural glen,

The breathing came from those bodies, long-warless, grown whiter than
     curds.

The wood was so spacious above them, that He who had stars for His flocks

Could fondle the leaves with His fingers, nor go from His dew-cumbered
     skies;

So long were they sleeping, the owls had builded their nests in their locks,

Filling the fibrous dimness with long generations of eyes.

And over the limbs and the valley the slow owls wandered and came,

Now in a place of star-fire, and now in a shadow place wide;

And the chief of the huge white creatures, his knees in the soft star-flame,

Lay loose in a place of shadow: we drew the reins by his side.

Golden the nails of his bird-claws, flung loosely along the dim ground;

In one was a branch soft-shining, with bells more many than sighs,

In midst of an old man's bosom; owls ruffling and pacing around,

Sidled their bodies against him, filling the shade with their eyes.

And my gaze was thronged with the sleepers; for nowhere in any clann

Of the high people of Soraca nor in glamour by demons flung,

Are faces alive with such beauty made known to the salt eye of man,

Yet weary with passions that faded when the sevenfold seas were young.

And I gazed on the bell-branch, sleep's forebear, far sung by the Sennachies.

I saw how those slumberers, grown weary, there camping in grasses deep,

Of wars with the wide world and pacing the shores of the wandering seas,

Laid hands on the bell-branch and swayed it, and fed of unhuman sleep.

Snatching the horn of Niamh, I blew a lingering note;

Came sound from those monstrous sleepers, a sound like the stirring of flies.

He, shaking the fold of his lips, and heaving the pillar of his throat,

Watched me with mournful wonder out of the wells of his eyes.

I cried, 'Come out of the shadow, king of the nails of gold!

And tell of your goodly household and the goodly works of your hands,

That we may muse in the starlight and talk of the battles of old;

Your questioner, Oisin, is worthy, he comes from the Fenian lands.'

Half open his eyes were, and held me, dull with the smoke of their dreams;

His lips moved slowly in answer, no answer out of them came;

Then he swayed in his fingers the bell-branch, slow dropping a sound in faint streams

Softer than snow-flakes in April and piercing the marrow like flame.

Wrapt in the wave of that music, with weariness more than of earth,

The moil of my centuries filled me; and gone like a sea-covered stone

Were the memories of the whole of my sorrow and the memories of the whole of my mirth,

And a softness came from the starlight and filled me full to the bone.

In the roots of the grasses, the sorrels, I laid my body as low;

And the pearl-pale Niamh lay by me, her brow on the midst of my breast;

And the horse was gone in the distance, and years after years 'gan flow;

Square leaves of the ivy moved over us, binding us down to our rest.

And, man of the many white croziers, a century there I forgot;

How the fetlocks drip blood in the battle, when the fallen on fallen lie rolled;

How the falconer follows the falcon in the weeds of the heron's plot,

And the names of the demons whose hammers made armour for Midhir of old.

And, man of the many white croziers, a century there I forgot;

That the spearshaft is made out of ashwood, the shield out of osier and hide;

How the hammers spring on the anvil, on the spear-head's burning spot;

How the slow, blue-eyed oxen of Finn low sadly at evening tide.

But in dreams, mild man of the croziers, driving the dust with their throngs,

Moved round me, of seamen or landsmen, all who are winter tales;

Came by me the Kings of the Red Branch, with roaring of laughter and songs,

Or moved as they moved once, love-making or piercing the tempest with sails.

Came Blanid, MacNessa, tall Fergus who feastward of old time slunk;

Cook Barach, the traitor; and warward, the spittle on his beard never dry,

Dark Balor, as old as a forest, car-borne, his mighty head sunk

Helpless, men lifting the lids of his weary and death-making eye.

And by me, in soft red raiment, the Fenians moved in loud streams,

And Grania, walking and smiling, sewed with her needle of bone.

So lived I and lived not, so wrought I and wrought not, with creatures of dreams,

In a long iron sleep, as a fish in the water goes dumb as a stone.

At times our slumber was lightened. When the sun was on silver or gold;

When brushed with the wings of the owls, in the dimness they love going by;

When a glow-worm was green on a grass leaf lured from his lair in the mould;

Half wakening, we lifted our eyelids, and gazed on the grass with a sigh.

So watched I when, man of the croziers, at the heel of a century fell,

Weak, in the midst of the meadow, from his miles in the midst of the air,

A starling like them that forgathered 'neath a moon waking white as a shell,

When the Fenians made foray at morning with Bran, Sgeolan, Lomair.

I awoke: the strange horse without summons out of the distance ran,

Thrusting his nose to my shoulder; he knew in his bosom deep

That once more moved in my bosom the ancient sadness of man,

And that I would leave the immortals, their dimness, their dews dropping sleep.

O, had you seen beautiful Niamh grow white as the waters are white,

Lord of the croziers, you even had lifted your hands and wept:

But, the bird in my fingers, I mounted, remembering alone that delight

Of twilight and slumber were gone, and that hoofs impatiently stept.

I cried, 'O Niamh! O white one! if only a twelve-houred day,

I must gaze on the beard of Finn, and move where the old men and young

In the Fenians' dwellings of wattle lean on the chessboards and play,

Ah, sweet to me now were even bald Conan's slanderous tongue!

'Like me were some galley forsaken far off in Meridian isle,

Remembering its long-oared companions, sails turning to thread-bare rags;

No more to crawl on the seas with long oars mile after mile,

But to be amid shooting of flies and flowering of rushes and flags.'

Their motionless eyeballs of spirits grown mild with mysterious thought,

Watched her those seamless faces from the valley's glimmering girth;

As she murmured, 'O wandering Oisin, the strength of the bell-branch is naught,

For there moves alive in your fingers the fluttering sadness of earth.

'Then go through the lands in the saddle and see what the mortals do,

And softly come to your Niamh over the tops of the tide;

But weep for your Niamh, O Oisin, weep; for if only your shoe

Brush lightly as haymouse earth pebbles, you will come no more to my side.

'O flaming lion of the world, O when will you turn to your rest?'

I saw from a distant saddle; from the earth she made her moan;

'I would die like a small withered leaf in the autumn, for breast unto breast

We shall mingle no more, nor our gazes empty their sweetness lone

'In the isles of the farthest seas where only the spirits come.

Were the winds less soft than the breath of a pigeon who sleeps on her nest,

Nor lost in the star-fires and odours the sound of the sea's vague drum,

O flaming lion of the world, O when will you turn to your rest?'

The wailing grew distant; I rode by the woods of the wrinkling bark,

Where ever is murmurous dropping, old silence and that one sound;

For no live creatures live there, no weasels move in the dark;

In a reverie forgetful of all things, over the bubbling ground.

And I rode by the plains of the sea's edge, where all is barren and gray,

Gray sands on the green of the grasses and over the dripping trees,

Dripping and doubling landward, as though they would hasten away,

Like an army of old men longing for rest from the moan of the seas.

And the winds made the sands on the sea's edge turning and turning go,

As my mind made the names of the Fenians. Far from the hazel and oak

I rode away on the surges, where, high as the saddle bow,

Fled foam underneath me, and round me, a wandering and milky smoke.

Long fled the foam-flakes around me, the winds fled out of the vast,

Snatching the bird in secret; nor knew I, embosomed apart,

When they froze the cloth on my body like armour riveted fast,

For Remembrance, lifting her leanness, keened in the gates of my heart.

Till fattening the winds of the morning, an odour of new-mown hay

Came, and my forehead fell low, and my tears like berries fell down;

Later a sound came, half lost in the sound of a shore far away,

From the great grass-barnacle calling, and later the shore-weeds brown.

If I were as I once was, the strong hoofs crushing the sand and the shells,

Coming out of the sea as the dawn comes, a chaunt of love on my lips,

Not coughing, my head on my knees, and praying, and wroth with the bells,

I would leave no saint's head on his body from Rachlin to Bera of ships.

Making way from the kindling surges, I rode on a bridle-path

Much wondering to see upon all hands, of wattles and woodwork made,

Your bell-mounted churches, and guardless the sacred cairn and the rath,

And a small and feeble race stooping with mattock and spade.

Or weeding or ploughing with faces a-shining with much-toil wet;

While in this place and that place, with bodies unglorious, their chieftains
stood,

Awaiting in patience the straw-death, croziered one, caught in their net:

Went the laughter of scorn from my mouth like the roaring of wind in a wood.

And because I went by them so huge and so speedy with eyes so bright,

Came after the hard gaze of youth, or an old man lifted his head:

And I rode and I rode, and I cried out, 'The Fenians hunt wolves in the night,

So sleep they by daytime.' A voice cried, 'The Fenians a long time are dead.'

A whitebeard stood hushed on the pathway, the flesh of his face as dried
grass,

And in folds round his eyes and his mouth, he sad as a child without milk;

And the dreams of the islands were gone, and I knew how men sorrow and
pass,

And their hound, and their horse, and their love, and their eyes that glimmer
like silk.

And wrapping my face in my hair, I murmured, 'In old age they ceased';

And my tears were larger than berries, and I murmured, 'Where white clouds
lie spread

On Crevroe or broad Knockfefin, with many of old they feast

On the floors of the gods.' He cried, 'No, the gods a long time are dead.'

And lonely and longing for Niamh, I shivered and turned me about,

The heart in me longing to leap like a grasshopper into her heart;

I turned and rode to the westward, and followed the sea's old shout

Till I saw where Maeve lies sleeping till starlight and midnight part.

And there at the foot of the mountain, two carried a sack full of sand,

They bore it with staggering and sweating, but fell with their burden at length:

Leaning down from the gem-studded saddle, I flung it five yards with my
hand,

With a sob for men waxing so weakly, a sob for the Fenians' old strength.

The rest you have heard of, O croziered one; how, when divided the girth,

I fell on the path, and the horse went away like a summer fly;

And my years three hundred fell on me, and I rose, and walked on the earth,

A creeping old man, full of sleep, with the spittle on his beard never dry.

How the men of the sand-sack showed me a church with its belfry in air;

Sorry place, where for swing of the war-axe in my dim eyes the crozier
    gleams;

What place have Caolte and Conan, and Bran, Sgeolan, Lomair?

Speak, you too are old with your memories, an old man surrounded with
    dreams.

S. PATRIC.

Where the flesh of the footsole clingeth on the burning stones is their place;

Where the demons whip them with wires on the burning stones of wide hell,

Watching the blessed ones move far off, and the smile on God's face,

Between them a gateway of brass, and the howl of the angels who fell.

OISIN.

Put the staff in my hands; for I go to the Fenians, O cleric, to chaunt

The war-songs that roused them of old; they will rise, making clouds with
    their breath

Innumerable, singing, exultant; the clay underneath them shall pant,

And demons be broken in pieces, and trampled beneath them in death.

And demons afraid in their darkness; deep horror of eyes and of wings,

Afraid their ears on the earth laid, shall listen and rise up and weep;

Hearing the shaking of shields and the quiver of stretched bowstrings,

Hearing hell loud with a murmur, as shouting and mocking we sweep.

We will tear out the flaming stones, and batter the gateway ofbrass

And enter, and none sayeth 'No' when there enters the strongly armed guest;

Make clean as a broom cleans, and march on as oxen move over young grass;

Then feast, making converse of Eire, of wars, and of old wounds, and rest.

S. PATRIC.

On the flaming stones, without refuge, the limbs of the Fenians are tost;

None war on the masters of Hell, who could break up the world in their rage;

But kneel and wear out the flags and pray for your soul that is lost

Through the demon love of its youth and its godless and passionate age.

OISIN.

Ah, me! to be shaken with coughing and broken with old age and pain,
Without laughter, a show unto children, alone with remembrance and fear,
All emptied of purple hours as a beggar's cloak in the rain,
As a grass seed crushed by a pebble, as a wolf sucked under a weir.
It were sad to gaze on the blessed and no man I loved of old there;
I throw down the chain of small stones! when life in my body has ceased,
I will go to Caolte, and Conan, and Bran, Sgeolan, Lomair,
And dwell in the house of the Fenians, be they in flames or at feast.

NOTES

THE WIND AMONG THE REEDS.

When I wrote these poems I had so meditated over the images that came to me in writing 'Ballads and Lyrics,' 'The Rose,' and 'The Wanderings of Oisin,' and other images from Irish folk-lore, that they had become true symbols. I had sometimes when awake, but more often in sleep, moments of vision, a state very unlike dreaming, when these images took upon themselves what seemed an independent life and became a part of a mystic language, which seemed always as if it would bring me some strange revelation. Being troubled at what was thought a reckless obscurity, I tried to explain myself in lengthy notes, into which I put all the little learning I had, and more wilful phantasy than I now think admirable, though what is most mystical still seems to me the most true. I quote in what follows the better or the more necessary passages.

THE HOSTING OF THE SIDHE (page 3).

The gods of ancient Ireland, the Tuatha De Danaan, or the Tribes of the goddess Danu, or the Sidhe, from Aes Sidhe, or Sluagh Sidhe, the people of the Faery Hills, as these words are usually explained, still ride the country as of old. Sidhe is also Gaelic for wind, and certainly the Sidhe have much to do with the wind. They journey in whirling winds, the winds that were called the dance of the daughters of Herodias in the Middle Ages, Herodias doubtless taking the place of some old goddess. When the country people see the leaves whirling on the road they bless themselves, because they believe the Sidhe to be passing by. They are almost always said to wear no covering upon their heads, and to let their hair stream out; and the great among them, for they have great and simple, go much upon horseback. If any one becomes too much interested in them, and sees them overmuch, he loses all interest in ordinary things.

A woman near Gort, in Galway, says: 'There is a boy, now, of the Clorans; but I wouldn't for the world let them think I spoke of him; it's two years since he came from America, and since that time he never went to Mass, or to church, or to fairs, or to market, or to stand on the cross roads, or to hurling, or to nothing. And if any one comes into the house, it's into the room he'll slip, not to see them; and as to work, he has the garden dug to bits, and the whole place smeared with cow dung; and such a crop as was never seen; and the alders all plaited till they look grand. One day he went as far as the chapel; but as soon as he got to the door he turned straight round again, as if he hadn't power to pass it. I wonder he wouldn't get the priest to read a Mass for him, or something; but the crop he has is grand, and you may know well he has some to help him.' One hears many stories of the kind; and a man whose son is believed to go out riding among them at night tells me that he is careless about everything, and lies in bed until it is late in the day. A doctor believes this boy to be mad. Those that are at times 'away,' as it is called, know all things, but are afraid to speak. A countryman at Kiltartan says, 'There was one of the Lydons—John—was away for seven years, lying in his bed, but brought away at nights, and he knew everything; and one, Kearney, up in the mountains, a cousin of his own, lost two hoggets, and came and told him, and he knew the very spot where they were, and told him, and he got them back again. But *they* were vexed at that, and took away the power, so that he never knew anything again, no more than another.'

Knocknarea is in Sligo, and the country people say that Maeve, still a great queen of the western Sidhe, is buried in the cairn of stones upon it. I have written of Clooth-na-Bare in 'The Celtic Twilight.' She 'went all over the world, seeking a lake deep enough to drown her faery life, of which she had grown weary, leaping from hill to hill, and setting up a cairn of stones wherever her feet lighted, until, at last, she found the deepest water in the world in little Lough Ia, on the top of the bird mountain, in Sligo.' I forget, now, where I heard this story, but it may have been from a priest at Collooney. Clooth-na-Bare would mean the old woman of Bare, but is evidently a corruption of Cailleac Bare, the old woman of Bare, who, under the names Bare, and Berah, and Beri, and Verah, and Dera, and Dhira, appears in the legends of many places. Mr. O'Grady found her haunting Lough Liath high up on the top of a mountain of the Fews, the Slieve Fuadh, or Slieve G- Cullain of old times, under the name of the Cailleac Buillia. He describes Lough Liath as a desolate moon-shaped lake, with made wells and sunken passages upon its borders, and beset by marsh and heather and gray boulders, and closes his 'Flight of the Eagle' with a long rhapsody upon mountain and lake, because of the heroic tales and beautiful old myths that have hung about them always. He identifies the Cailleac Buillia with that Meluchra who persuaded Fionn to go to her amid the waters of Lough Liath, and so changed him with her enchantments, that, though she had to free him because of the threats of the Fiana, his hair was ever afterwards as white as snow. To this day the Tuatha De Danaan that are in the waters beckon to men, and drown them in the waters; and Bare, or Dhira, or Meluchra, or whatever name one likes the best, is, doubtless, the name of a mistress among them. Meluchra was daughter of Cullain; and Cullain Mr. O'Grady calls, upon I know not what authority, a form of Lir, the master of waters. The people of the waters have been in all ages beautiful and changeable and lascivious, or beautiful and wise and lonely, for water is everywhere the signature of the fruitfulness of the body and of the fruitfulness of dreams. The white hair of Fionn may be but another of the troubles of those that come to unearthly wisdom and earthly trouble, and the threats and violence of the Fiana against her, a different form of the threats and violence the country people use, to make the Aes Sidhe give up those that are 'away.' Bare is now often called an ugly old woman, but in the 'Song of Bare,' which Lady Gregory has given in her 'Saints and Wonders,' she laments her lost beauty after the withering of seven hundred years; and Dr. Joyce says that one of her old names was Aebhin, which means beautiful. Aebhin was the goddess of the tribes of northern Leinster; and the lover she had made immortal, and who loved her perfectly, left her, and put on mortality, to fight among them against the stranger, and died on the strand of Clontarf.

THE POET PLEADS WITH THE ELEMENTAL POWERS (p. 37). HE THINKS OF HIS PAST GREATNESS WHEN A PART OF THE CONSTELLATIONS OF HEAVEN (p. 40). HE HEARS THE CRY OF THE SEDGE (p. 28).

The Rose has been for many centuries a symbol of spiritual love and supreme beauty. The lotus was in some Eastern countries imagined blossoming upon the Tree of Life, as the Flower of Life, and is thus represented in Assyrian bas-reliefs. Because the Rose, the flower sacred to the Virgin Mary, and the flower that Apuleius' adventurer ate, when he was changed out of the ass's shape and received into the fellowship of Isis, is the western Flower of Life, I have imagined it growing upon the Tree of Life. I once stood beside a man in Ireland when he saw it growing there in a vision, that seemed to have rapt him out of his body. He saw the Garden of Eden walled about, and on the top of a high mountain, as in certain mediæval diagrams, and after passing the Tree of Knowledge, on which grew fruit full of troubled faces, and through whose branches flowed, he was told, sap that was human souls, he came to a tall, dark tree, with little bitter fruits, and was shown a kind of stair or ladder going up through the tree, and told to go up; and near the top of the tree, a beautiful woman, like the Goddess of Life, associated with the tree in Assyria, gave him a rose that seemed to have been growing upon the tree. One finds the Rose in the Irish poets, sometimes as a religious symbol, as in the phrase, 'the Rose of Friday,' meaning the Rose of austerity, in a Gaelic poem in Dr. Hyde's 'Religious Songs of Connacht'; and, I think, as a symbol of woman's beauty in the Gaelic song, 'Roseen Dubh'; and a symbol of Ireland in Mangan's adaptation of 'Roseen Dubh,' 'My Dark Rosaleen,' and in Mr. Aubrey de Vere's 'The Little Black Rose.' I do not know any evidence to prove whether this symbol came to Ireland with mediæval Christianity, or whether it has come down from older times. I have read somewhere that a stone engraved with a Celtic god, who holds what looks like a rose in one hand, has been found somewhere in England; but I cannot find the reference, though I certainly made a note of it. If the Rose was really a symbol of Ireland among the Gaelic poets, and if 'Roseen Dubh' is really a political poem, as some think, one may feel pretty certain that the ancient Celts associated the Rose with Eire, or Fotla, or Banba—goddesses who gave their names to Ireland—or with some principal god or goddess, for such symbols are not suddenly adopted or invented, but come out of mythology.

I have made the Seven Lights, the constellation of the Bear, lament for the theft of the Rose, and I have made the Dragon, the constellation Draco, the guardian of the Rose, because these constellations move about the pole of the heavens, the ancient Tree of Life in many countries, and are often associated with the Tree of Life in mythology. It is this Tree of Life that I have put into the 'Song of Mongan' under its common Irish form of a hazel; and, because it had sometimes the stars for fruit, I have hung upon it 'the Crooked Plough' and the 'Pilot Star,' as Gaelic-speaking Irishmen sometimes call the Bear and the North star. I have made it an axle-tree in 'Aedh hears the Cry of the Sedge,' for this was another ancient way of representing it.

THE HOST OF THE AIR (p. 6).

Some writers distinguish between the Sluagh Gaoith, the host of the air, and Sluagh Sidhe, the host of the Sidhe, and describe the host of the air as of a peculiar malignancy. Dr. Joyce says, 'Of all the different kinds of goblins… . air demons were most dreaded by the people. They lived among clouds, and mists, and rocks, and hated the human race with the utmost malignity.' A very old Aran charm, which contains the words 'Send God, by his strength, between us and the host of the Sidhe, between us and the host of the air,' seems also to distinguish among them. I am inclined, however, to think that the distinction came in with Christianity and its belief about the prince of the air, for the host of the Sidhe, as I have already explained, are closely associated with the wind.

They are said to steal brides just after their marriage, and sometimes in a blast of wind. A man in Galway says, 'At Aughanish there were two couples came to the shore to be married, and one of the newly married women was in the boat with the priest, and they going back to the island; and a sudden blast of wind came, and the priest said some blessed words that were able to save himself, but the girl was swept.'

This woman was drowned; but more often the persons who are taken 'get the touch,' as it is called, and fall into a half dream, and grow indifferent to all things, for their true life has gone out of the world, and is among the hills and the forts of the Sidhe. A faery doctor has told me that his wife 'got the touch' at her marriage because there was one of them wanted her; and the way he knew for certain was, that when he took a pitchfork out of the rafters, and told her it was a broom, she said, 'It is a broom.' She was, the truth is, in the magical sleep, to which people have given a new name lately, that makes the imagination so passive that it can be moulded by any voice in any world into any shape. A mere likeness of some old woman, or even old animal, some one or some thing the Sidhe have no longer a use for, is believed to be left instead of the person who is 'away'; this some one or some thing can, it is thought, be driven away by threats, or by violence (though I have heard country women say that violence is wrong), which perhaps awakes the soul out of the magical sleep. The story in the poem is founded on an old Gaelic ballad that was sung and translated for me by a woman at Ballisodare in County Sligo; but in the ballad the husband found the keeners keening his wife when he got to his house. She was 'swept' at once; but the Sidhe are said to value those the most whom they but cast into a half dream, which may last for years, for they need the help of a living person in most of the things they do. There are many stories of people who seem to die and be buried—though the country people will tell you it is but some one or some thing put in their place that dies and is buried—and yet are brought back afterwards. These tales are perhaps memories of true awakenings out of the magical sleep, moulded by the imagination, under the influence of a mystical doctrine which it understands too literally, into the shape of some well-known traditional tale. One does not hear them as one hears the others, from the persons who are 'away,' or from their wives or husbands; and one old man, who had often seen the Sidhe, began one of them with 'Maybe it is all vanity.'

Here is a tale that a friend of mine heard in the Burren hills, and it is a type of all:—

'There was a girl to be married, and she didn't like the man, and she cried when the day was coming, and said she wouldn't go along with him. And the mother said, "Get into the bed, then, and I'll say that you're sick." And so she did. And when the man came the mother said to him, "You can't get her, she's sick in the bed." And he looked in and said, "That's not my wife that's in the bed, it's some old hag." And the mother began to cry and roar. And he went out and got two hampers of turf, and made a fire, that they thought he was going to burn the house down. And when the fire was kindled, "Come out, now," says he, "and we'll see who you are, when I'll put you on the fire." And when she heard that, she gave one leap, and was out of the house, and they saw, then, it was an old hag she was. Well, the man asked the advice of an old woman, and she bid him go to a faery-bush that was near, and he might get some word of her. So he went there at night, and saw all sorts of grand people, and they in carriages or riding on horses, and among them he could

163

see the girl he came to look for. So he went again to the old woman, and she said, "If you can get the three bits of blackthorn out of her hair, you'll get her again." So that night he went again, and that time he only got hold of a bit of her hair. But the old woman told him that was no use, and that he was put back now, and it might be twelve nights before he'd get her. But on the fourth night he got the third bit of blackthorn, and he took her, and she came away with him. He never told the mother he had got her; but one day she saw her at a fair, and, says she, "That's my daughter; I know her by the smile and by the laugh of her, and she with a shawl about her head." So the husband said, "You're right there, and hard I worked to get her." She spoke often of the grand things she saw underground, and how she used to have wine to drink, and to drive out in a carriage with four horses every night. And she used to be able to see her husband when he came to look for her, and she was greatly afraid he'd get a drop of the wine, for then he would have come underground and never left it again. And she was glad herself to come to earth again, and not to be left there.'

The old Gaelic literature is full of the appeals of the Tuatha De Danaan to mortals whom they would bring into their country; but the song of Midher to the beautiful Etain, the wife of the king who was called Echaid the ploughman, is the type of all.

'O beautiful woman, come with me to the marvellous land where one listens to a sweet music, where one has spring flowers in one's hair, where the body is like snow from head to foot, where no one is sad or silent, where teeth are white and eyebrows are black… cheeks red like foxglove in flower… . Ireland is beautiful, but not so beautiful as the Great Plain I call you to. The beer of Ireland is heady, but the beer of the Great Plain is much more heady. How marvellous is the country I am speaking of! Youth does not grow old there. Streams with warm flood flow there; sometimes mead, sometimes wine. Men are charming and without a blot there, and love is not forbidden there. O woman, when you come into my powerful country you will wear a crown of gold upon your head. I will give you the flesh of swine, and you will have beer and milk to drink, O beautiful woman. O beautiful woman, come with me!'

THE SONG OF WANDERING AENGUS (p. 11).

The Tuatha De Danaan can take all shapes, and those that are in the waters take often the shape of fish. A woman of Burren, in Galway, says, 'There are more of them in the sea than on the land, and they sometimes try to come over the side of the boat in the form of fishes, for they can take their choice shape.' At other times they are beautiful women; and another Galway woman says,

'Surely those things are in the sea as well as on land. My father was out fishing one night off Tyrone. And something came beside the boat that had eyes shining like candles. And then a wave came in, and a storm rose all in a minute, and whatever was in the wave, the weight of it had like to sink the boat. And then they saw that it was a woman in the sea that had the shining eyes. So my father went to the priest, and he bid him always to take a drop of holy water and a pinch of salt out in the boat with him, and nothing could harm him.'

The poem was suggested to me by a Greek folk song; but the folk belief of Greece is very like that of Ireland, and I certainly thought, when I wrote it, of Ireland, and of the spirits that are in Ireland. An old man who was cutting a quickset hedge near Gort, in Galway, said, only the other day, 'One time I was cutting timber over in Inchy, and about eight o'clock one morning, when I got there, I saw a girl picking nuts, with her hair hanging down over her shoulders; brown hair; and she had a good, clean face, and she was tall, and nothing on her head, and her dress no way gaudy, but simple. And when she felt me coming she gathered herself up, and was gone, as if the earth had swallowed her up. And I followed her, and looked for her, but I never could see her again from that day to this, never again.'

The county Galway people use the word 'clean' in its old sense of fresh and comely.

HE MOURNS FOR THE CHANGE THAT HAS COME UPON HIM AND HIS BELOVED, AND LONGS FOR THE END OF THE WORLD (p. 15).

My deer and hound are properly related to the deer and hound that flicker in and out of the various tellings of the Arthurian legends, leading different knights upon adventures, and to the hounds and to the hornless deer at the beginning of, I think, all tellings of Oisin's journey to the country of the young. The hound is certainly related to the Hounds of Annwvyn or of Hades, who are white, and have red ears, and were heard, and are, perhaps, still heard by Welsh peasants, following some flying thing in the night winds; and is probably related to the hounds that Irish country people believe will awake and seize the souls of the dead if you lament them too loudly or too soon. An old woman told a friend and myself that she saw what she thought were white birds, flying over an enchanted place; but found, when she got near, that they had dogs' heads, and I do not doubt that my hound and these dog-headed birds are of the same family. I got my hound and deer out of a last century Gaelic poem about Oisin's journey to the country of the young. After the hunting of the hornless deer, that leads him to the seashore, and while he is riding over the sea with Niamh, he sees amid the waters—I have not the

Gaelic poem by me, and describe it from memory—a young man following a girl who has a golden apple, and afterwards a hound with one red ear following a deer with no horns. This hound and this deer seem plain images of the desire of man 'which is for the woman,' and 'the desire of the woman which is for the desire of the man,' and of all desires that are as these. I have read them in this way in 'The Wanderings of Usheen' or Oisin, and have made my lover sigh because he has seen in their faces 'the immortal desire of immortals.'

The man in my poem who has a hazel wand may have been Aengus, Master of Love; and I have made the boar without bristles come out of the West, because the place of sunset was in Ireland, as in other countries, a place of symbolic darkness and death.

THE CAP AND BELLS (p. 22).

I dreamed this story exactly as I have written it, and dreamed another long dream after it, trying to make out its meaning, and whether I was to write it in prose or verse. The first dream was more a vision than a dream, for it was beautiful and coherent, and gave me the sense of illumination and exaltation that one gets from visions, while the second dream was confused and meaningless. The poem has always meant a great deal to me, though, as is the way with symbolic poems, it has not always meant quite the same thing. Blake would have said, 'the authors are in eternity,' and I am quite sure they can only be questioned in dreams.

THE VALLEY OF THE BLACK PIG (p. 24).

All over Ireland there are prophecies of the coming rout of the enemies of Ireland, in a certain Valley of the Black Pig, and these prophecies are, no doubt, now, as they were in the Fenian days, a political force. I have heard of one man who would not give any money to the Land League, because the Battle could not be until the close of the century; but, as a rule, periods of trouble bring prophecies of its near coming. A few years before my time, an old man who lived at Lisadill, in Sligo, used to fall down in a fit and rave out descriptions of the Battle; and a man in Sligo has told me that it will be so great a battle that the horses shall go up to their fetlocks in blood, and that their girths, when it is over, will rot from their bellies for lack of a hand to unbuckle them. If one reads Professor Rhys' "Celtic Heathendom" by the light of Professor Frazer's "Golden Bough," and puts together what one finds there about the boar that killed Diarmuid, and other old Celtic boars and sows, one sees that the battle is mythological, and that the Pig it is named from must be a type of cold and winter doing battle with the summer, or of death battling with life. For the purposes of poetry, at any rate, I think it a symbol of the darkness that will destroy the world. The country people say there is no shape for a spirit to take so dangerous as the shape of a pig; and a Galway blacksmith—and blacksmiths are thought to be specially protected—says he would be afraid to meet a pig on the road at night; and another Galway man tells this story: 'There was a man coming the road from Gort to Garryland one night, and he had a drop taken; and before him, on the road, he saw a pig walking; and having a drop in, he gave a shout, and made a kick at it, and bid it get out of that. And by the time he got home, his arm was swelled from the shoulder to be as big as a bag, and he couldn't use his hand with the pain of it. And his wife brought him, after a few days, to a woman that used to do cures at Rahasane. And on the road all she could do would hardly keep him from lying down to sleep on the grass. And when they got to the woman she knew all that happened; "and," says she, "it's well for you that your wife didn't let you fall asleep on the grass, for if you had done that but even for one instant, you'd be a lost man."'

Professor Rhys, who considers the bristleless boar a symbol of darkness and cold, rather than of winter and cold, thinks it was without bristles because the darkness is shorn away by the sun.

The Battle should, I believe, be compared with three other battles; a battle the Sidhe are said to fight when a person is being taken away by them; a battle they are said to fight in November for the harvest; the great battle the Tuatha De Danaan fought, according to the Gaelic chroniclers, with the Fomor at Moy Tura, or the Towery Plain.

I have heard of the battle over the dying both in County Galway and in the Isles of Aran, an old Aran fisherman having told me that it was fought over two of his children, and that he found blood in a box he had for keeping fish, when it was over; and I have written about it, and given examples elsewhere. A faery doctor, on the borders of Galway and Clare, explained it as a battle between the friends and enemies of the dying, the one party trying to take them, the other trying to save them from being taken. It may once, when the land of the Sidhe was the only other world, and when every man who died was carried thither, have always accompanied death. I suggest that the battle between the Tuatha De Danaan, the powers of light, and warmth, and fruitfulness, and goodness, and the Fomor, the powers of darkness, and cold, and barrenness, and badness upon the Towery Plain, was the establishment of the habitable world, the rout of the ancestral darkness; that the battle among the Sidhe for the harvest is the annual battle of summer and winter; that the battle among the Sidhe at a man's death is the battle of life and death; and that the battle of the Black Pig is the battle between the manifest world and the ancestral darkness at the end of all things; and that all these battles are one, the battle of all things with shadowy decay. Once a symbolism has possessed the imagination of large numbers of men, it becomes, as I believe, an embodiment of disembodied powers, and repeats itself in dreams and visions, age after age.

The Secret Rose (p. 32).

I find that I have unintentionally changed the old story of Conchubar's death. He did not see the crucifixion in a vision, but was told about it. He had been struck by a ball, made of the dried brain of a dead enemy, and hurled out of a sling; and this ball had been left in his head, and his head had been mended, the 'Book of Leinster' says, with thread of gold because his hair was like gold. Keating, a writer of the time of Elizabeth, says, 'In that state did he remain seven years, until the Friday on which Christ was crucified, according to some historians; and when he saw the unusual changes of the creation and the eclipse of the sun and the moon at its full, he asked of Bucrach, a Leinster Druid, who was along with him, what was it that brought that unusual change upon the planets of Heaven and Earth. "Jesus Christ, the Son of God," said the Druid, "who is now being crucified by the Jews." "That is a pity," said Conchubar; "were I in his presence I would kill those who were putting him to death." And with that he brought out his sword, and rushed at a woody grove which was convenient to him, and began to cut and fell it; and what he said was, that if he were among the Jews, that was the usage he would give them, and from the excessiveness of his fury which seized upon him, the ball started out of his head, and some of the brain came after it, and in that way he died. The wood of Lanshraigh, in Feara Rois, is the name by which that shrubby wood is called.'

I have imagined Cuchulain meeting Fand 'walking among flaming dew.' The story of their love is one of the most beautiful of our old tales.

I have founded the man 'who drove the gods out of their Liss,' or fort, upon something I have read about Caolte after the battle of Gabra, when almost all his companions were killed, driving the gods out of their Liss, either at Osraighe, now Ossory, or at Eas Ruaidh, now Asseroe, a waterfall at Ballyshannon, where Ilbreac, one of the children of the goddess Danu, had a Liss. But maybe I only read it in Mr. Standish O'Grady, who has a fine imagination, for I find no such story in Lady Gregory's book.

I have founded 'the proud dreaming king' upon Fergus, the son of Roigh, the legendary poet of 'the quest of the bull of Cuailgne,' as he is in the ancient story of Deirdre, and in modern poems by Ferguson. He married Nessa, and Ferguson makes him tell how she took him 'captive in a single look.'

'I am but an empty shade,

Far from life and passion laid;

Yet does sweet remembrance thrill

All my shadowy being still.'

Presently, because of his great love, he gave up his throne to Conchubar, her son by another, and lived out his days feasting, and fighting, and hunting. His promise never to refuse a feast from a certain comrade, and the mischief that came by his promise, and the vengeance he took afterwards, are a principal theme of the poets. I have explained my changing imaginations of him in 'Fergus and the Druid,' and in a little song in the second act of 'The Countess Kathleen,' and in 'Deirdre.'

I have founded him 'who sold tillage, and house, and goods,' upon something in 'The Red Pony,' a folk tale in Mr. Larminie's 'West Irish Folk Tales.' A young man 'saw a light before him on the high road. When he came as far, there was an open box on the road, and a light coming up out of it. He took up the box. There was a lock of hair in it. Presently he had to go to become the servant of a king for his living. There were eleven boys. When they were going out into the stable at ten o'clock, each of them took a light but he. He took no candle at all with him. Each of them went into his own stable. When he went into his stable he opened the box. He left it in a hole in the wall. The light was great. It was twice as much as in the other stables.' The king hears of it, and makes him show him the box. The king says, 'You must go and bring me the woman to whom the hair belongs.' In the end, the young man, and not the king, marries the woman.

EARLY POEMS:

BALLADS AND LYRICS (<u>p. 89</u>). 'THE ROSE' (<u>p. 139</u>). 'THE WANDERINGS OF OISIN' (<u>p. 175</u>).

When I first wrote I went here and there for my subjects as my reading led me, and preferred to all other countries Arcadia and the India of romance, but presently I convinced myself, for such reasons as those in 'Ireland and the Arts,' that I should never go for the scenery of a poem to any country but my own, and I think that I shall hold to that conviction to the end. I was very young; and, perhaps because I belonged to a Young Ireland Society in Dublin, I wished to be as easily understood as the Young Ireland writers, to write always out of the common thought of the people.

I have put the poems written while I was influenced by this desire, though with an always lessening force, into those sections which I have called 'Early Poems.' I read certain of them now with no little discontent, for I find, especially in the ballads, some triviality and sentimentality. Mangan and Davis, at their best, are not sentimental and trivial, but I became so from an imitation that was not natural to me. When I was writing the poems in the second of the three, the section called 'The Rose,' I found that I was becoming unintelligible to the young men who had been in my thought. We have still the same tradition, but I have been like a traveller who, having when newly arrived in the city noticed nothing but the news of the market-place, the songs of the workmen, the great public buildings, has come after certain months to let his thoughts run upon some little carving in its niche, some Ogham on a stone, or the conversation of a countryman who knows more of the 'Boar without Bristles' than of the daily paper.

When writing I went for nearly all my subjects to Irish folklore and legends, much as a Young Ireland poet would have done, writing 'Down by the Salley Garden' by adding a few lines to a couple of lines I heard sung at Ballisodare; 'The Meditation of the Old Fisherman' from the words of a not very old fisherman at Rosses Point; 'The Lamentation of the Old Pensioner' from words spoken by a man on the Two Rock Mountain to a friend of mine; 'The Ballad of the Old Foxhunter' from an incident in one of Kickham's novels; and 'The Ballad of Moll Magee' from a sermon preached in a chapel at Howth; and 'The Wanderings of Oisin' from a Gaelic poem of the Eighteenth Century and certain Middle Irish poems in dialogue. It is no longer necessary to say who Oisin and Cuchulain and Fergus and the other bardic persons are, for Lady Gregory, in her 'Gods and Fighting Men' and 'Cuchulain of Muirthemne' has re-told all that is greatest in the ancient literature of Ireland in a style that has to my ears an immortal beauty.

Printed by A. H. Bᴜʟʟᴇɴ, *at The Shakespeare Head Press, Stratford-on-Avon.*